The Daredevil

Also From Dylan Allen

RIVERS WILDE SERIES OF STAND ALONE STORIES
Listed in suggested reading order

The Legacy
Book one of the Rivers Wilde Series. An opposites attract, enemies to lovers standalone that kicks off this brand new series.

The Legend
This is a second chance at love story. Remington Wilde has loved one woman in his life and even though timing and family manipulations keep pulling them apart, it's a love worth fighting for.

The Jezebel
Regan Wilde and Stone Rivers were born enemies. But love has other ideas. This sweeping, second chance romance spans nearly twenty years and will make you believe in soul mates.

The Daredevil: A Rivers Wilde/ 1001 Nights Novella
This story has all the hallmarks of Rivers Wilde—drama, sex, humor, heartwarming family interactions, and two amazingly driven, brilliant, bold characters who are also PERFECT for each other. A fake relationship, a weekend in Paris and all the feels.

SYMBOLS OF LOVE SERIES
Rise
Remember
Release

STANDALONE NOVELS
The Sun and Her Star
Thicker Than Water

The Daredevil

A Rivers Wilde Novella

By Dylan Allen

1001 DARK NIGHTS
PRESS

The Daredevil
A Rivers Wilde Novella
By Dylan Allen

1001 Dark Nights

Copyright 2021 Dylan Allen
ISBN: 978-1-951812-49-2

Foreword: Copyright 2014 M. J. Rose

Published by 1001 Dark Nights Press, an imprint of Evil Eye
Concepts, Incorporated

Sign up for the 1001 Dark Nights Newsletter
and be entered to win a Tiffany Key necklace.

There's a contest every month!

Go to www.1001DarkNights.com to subscribe.

**As a bonus, all subscribers can download
FIVE FREE exclusive books!**

Dedication

This book is dedicated to every dreamer who refuses to stay down,
And who never, ever stops believing.

Acknowledgments from the Author

The exercise of expressing gratitude is always such a life affirming exercise for me. When I sit to think about the people who made this book possible, I'm always so humbled by the fact that I have such an amazing village of people in my life who are not only rooting for me but are working and investing in my success.

I have to start by thanking Liz Berry, Jillian Greenfield-Stein, and M.J. Rose from 1001 Dark Nights for this amazing opportunity. The chance to write this story and join the 1001 Dark Nights family is one of the greatest honors of my career, and I will never stop pinching myself. I can't wait to do it again.

Every story I write goes through countless rounds of edits and rewrites, and I couldn't do that without my beta readers—Thank you to Chelé Walker (who is my alpha reader), Yolanda McGee, Zoe Braycotton, Tiffani Pruitt, and Ann Jones (I owe you all a massage for your help with this story), Ginger Scott (Thank you for not blocking me) and Jenn Watson (Your contribution can't be measured, love you, J!).

I've published 10 books and I've never had a better experience with a copyeditor than I did with Kasi Alexander, who made this book shine. Thank you for your patience, your attention to detail and your *PATIENCE*.

This writing job can feel like a lonely, hard slog, but it's made so much easier by the authors who are the constant gardeners of my inspiration and motivation—Kennedy, Brittainy, Kenya, Danielle, Nana, Giana Angel Payne, Tara, Ginger Scott, AL (Amy) Sandra, Melanie, Kayti, Laurelin, Penny, Lucy, LJ, Susie, Thandi, Nikki, and more I'm sure I'm missing—you are all so dear to me. Thank you for making the journey so much fun.

To my Melissa Panio-Petersen, who is the other half of Team Dylan, thank you for holding everything together and making my life so much easier. I am so grateful for all your hard work. Love you.

To my Dreamers all over the world who read my books, write me emails, hang out in my reader group—I write for you. And I always will.

To my amazing family who is the place from where all my blessings flow. I couldn't be without you and I count you as my biggest blessing. I love you.

Dream Big, Dreamers!
Love,
Dx.

One Thousand and One Dark Nights

Once upon a time, in the future…

*I was a student fascinated with stories and learning.
I studied philosophy, poetry, history, the occult, and
the art and science of love and magic. I had a vast
library at my father's home and collected thousands
of volumes of fantastic tales.*

*I learned all about ancient races and bygone
times. About myths and legends and dreams of all
people through the millennium. And the more I read
the stronger my imagination grew until I discovered
that I was able to travel into the stories… to actually
become part of them.*

*I wish I could say that I listened to my teacher
and respected my gift, as I ought to have. If I had, I
would not be telling you this tale now.
But I was foolhardy and confused, showing off
with bravery.*

*One afternoon, curious about the myth of the
Arabian Nights, I traveled back to ancient Persia to
see for myself if it was true that every day Shahryar
(Persian: شهريار, "king") married a new virgin, and then
sent yesterday's wife to be beheaded. It was written
and I had read that by the time he met Scheherazade,
the vizier's daughter, he'd killed one thousand
women.*

Something went wrong with my efforts. I arrived in the midst of the story and somehow exchanged places with Scheherazade – a phenomena that had never occurred before and that still to this day, I cannot explain.

Now I am trapped in that ancient past. I have taken on Scheherazade's life and the only way I can protect myself and stay alive is to do what she did to protect herself and stay alive.

Every night the King calls for me and listens as I spin tales. And when the evening ends and dawn breaks, I stop at a point that leaves him breathless and yearning for more. And so the King spares my life for one more day, so that he might hear the rest of my dark tale.

As soon as I finish a story... I begin a new one... like the one that you, dear reader, have before you now.

Introduction

Located in the dynamic city of Houston, TX, Rivers Wilde is an enclave carved into a parcel of the most valuable and coveted land in all of South East Texas.

The enclave is home to the two families that it's named after. The Rivers are old Texas money. Sugar, oil, and natural gas are how they made their fortune. And with that bounty, they helped found the city of Houston.

The Wildes are the new money. The *bourgeoisie*. They built their wealth in restaurants, grocery stores, and real estate. And they have made a fortune that casts the old money into the shade.

In the 1980s, the oil markets were crashing, and the Rivers found themselves hard up for cash. With no other viable options, they sold part of their precious land to the usurpers they'd previously refused to even acknowledge.

Seeds of resentment burrowed deep into the fertile soil of their dislike and grew tenacious roots. Thirty years later, the rivalry continues. Even though now no one remembers what started it and just *why* the blood between the families is so bad.

Today in Rivers Wilde, a new generation is coming to the helm of power in both families. Will they put the past behind them and usher in a new era of cooperation between the two ruling families in Houston? Or will the sins of their fathers continue to cast a shadow over them?

I hope you enjoy finding out!

Prologue

Birthright
Tyson

Roses remind me of death. For as long as I can remember, they were the only flowers we took to my father's tombstone on our monthly visits. That there's a bunch sitting in the vase next to the chair where I'm waiting to learn my fate only adds to the weight of impending doom that's been hanging over my neck like the Sword of Damocles.

My phone rings, and the name "Kayleigh" pops up on my screen. I immediately decline the call. She has a lot of fucking nerve calling me after what she's done.

And everything she could have cost me.

My mother has already made it clear that there will be repercussions for my lack of judgment and discretion, but her bark has always been worse than her bite. Not that this meeting she called is going to be great. But if her tongue was a knife, the riot act she read me would have flayed all the meat from my bones.

It's been nearly a week since that happened, and I can still feel the sting of her rebuke. So it's nice to know the worst is behind me. My mother is a hard, unyielding matriarch who fought her way from a life of poverty in Kingston, Jamaica to the head of one of the largest companies in the world. She didn't get there by cutting anyone, including herself, slack.

And the only soft spot she has is the place in her heart that belongs to me.

She has contentious relationships with both my siblings. She and my older brother, Remington, sometimes go months without speaking. But I've always been different.

In a family of overachievers, I've been considered the runt of the litter.

I still live in the shade cast by Remington, who was not only nicknamed The Legend, but was, in many ways, truly legendary. Basketball, law, life—he was great at all of it. My sister Regan was less outgoing but just as impressive as Remi. They're twins, born nearly five years before me.

My grandfather, may he burn in hell, used to say that they got all the good genes, and I got whatever was left.

I had a speech delay that I didn't shake until I was in eighth grade, asthma attacks that made emergency room visits a way of life, and team sports were a no-fly zone. When people invariably measured us against each other, I always came up short. It didn't help that I was born five months after my mother became a widow and had to step into the role her husband's death left empty at my family's rapidly expanding food retail service and real estate business.

When I was born, she didn't take a break from her career to raise me. Instead, she hired an army of nannies, drivers, cooks, and au pairs who made sure I was everywhere I needed to be.

But on the weekends, she never worked, and that was our time. We spent nearly every waking minute together from Friday night to Monday morning. I spent all week getting myself ready to impress her. I'd draw her pictures or memorize a poem and make a big show of presenting it. Even at that tender age, I understood my place in the hierarchy of her life.

The company came first, everything else got whatever she had left to give.

Wilde World was started by my great-grandfather as a grocery business. And for the first fifty years of its life, that's all it was. Not that it was anything to sniff at. By the time my parents got married, Wilde World was one of the largest grocers in the state of Texas

Until my father, spurred on by his ambitious, brilliant new wife, proposed that the company use its immense capital to buy a plot of land and build a subdivision on it.

It was the stuff of dreams, but my father was a brilliant salesman, and my mother was an even more brilliant business strategist.

My father didn't see his brainchild come to life. He died soon after the first tract of homeowners broke ground. And my grandfather, who was still ruling the company with an iron fist, didn't share the power with my mother the way my father would have. But she proved herself to be indispensable, and even though she didn't get the credit for it, I knew she was still the brains behind the operation.

I was fifteen when my grandfather suffered a stroke that forced him to retire, and my mother stepped up to the helm.

When she's interviewed, she always says that she was simply standing in my father's stead. But the truth is, she was born to build and lead, and if my father was alive, I'm sure he'd agree and let her.

Fifteen years of her leadership have seen Wilde go from a regional grocer to an international food service company.

At that point, she barely had time to say hello in the mornings, much less spend her weekends with me. But I'd tired of them by then, anyway.

I had a massive growth spurt when I was 14. I outgrew my asthma and made the straight A honor roll my freshman year of high school. I joined the track and field and football teams and started working out. For the first time in my life, I felt like I was in the body I was born in.

I felt ready to live up to my last name. Because all I wanted was to be a Wilde—in name *and* deed.

My older brother was the heir apparent, but I knew that he had his eye on a different prize. And when he chose to go to law school, abandoning the expectation that he'd run this company after my mother, I saw the opportunity and stepped up.

I've worked at Wilde since I was 14. By the time I graduated from college and started in a junior level marketing role, I was a bona fide workaholic. All work and no play made for a very dull life. Girls liked me, and I liked them back. Especially the older ones.

But I'd also let my brother's missteps when it came to women be a lesson, and I made sure my mother didn't catch a whiff of my relationships.

Until I let the lines between business and my personal life blur. I met a girl at happy hour at The Belvedere. When she told me she was in town interviewing for a position at Wilde World, I used my name to get her back to my place. Looking back now, I can see clearly how stupid I was. I helped her prep for her interview. She got the job, and for the workaholic in me, having her in the building meant I didn't need to leave the office for anything. I thought I was falling in love with her, and I trusted her. She offered to help me with a presentation I was giving for my first real attempt at landing an account on my own, and I gladly accepted.

I made my pitch, and when the company called me back, I was sure it was to tell me that they loved our presentation and wanted to do business. Instead, they informed me that the pitch I presented was identical to one given by a competitor just two days before. They believed I'd stolen their work and informed me that Wilde World would be blacklisted from doing business with them.

Going to my mother with that news last week was bad.

But finding out that Kayleigh was a plant from the competitor's company—that the whole thing, including bumping into each other that night, was a setup. That was the worst.

She swore it was only that way in the beginning. But I didn't believe anything she said.

"Tyson, Mrs. Wilde will see you now," my mother's assistant calls from behind her desk. I nod and walk on leaden legs into her office.

She's writing, head down, and I move to the chairs in front of her desk.

"Don't sit. This won't take long," she says in a monotone voice, her dark head still bent to her task.

"Okay."

She writes a few more words and then slams her leatherbound portfolio closed with a loud slap. She looks up at me, and the flash of steel in her eyes, the same dark as midnight color as mine, pierces me to the bone. "I have made a decision," she says, her voice still without intonation. "But first, I want to explain something to you."

I nod and brace myself for her rebuke.

"If you want to lead this company, you will have to put it first."

"I know. And I have."

She holds one red-tipped elegant finger up to silence me. "You have not, Tyson. But it's not your fault. I've lied to you about your father, and in doing so, I didn't allow you the benefit of learning from his mistakes."

The hairs on the back of my neck stand up, and what feels like an entire shiver of sharks start swimming in my stomach.

"What mistakes?" I ask. Because my father, Lucas Wilde, was the Patron Saint of Wilde World's dynasty.

A small smile lifts the left corner of her mouth, and her eyes lose their intensity. "Have you heard the phrase *Eternal sunshine of the spotless mind?*"

I'm at once confused and fucking terrified. I nod. "That's a movie, right?"

Her eyes narrow. "The movie's title comes from a poem by Alexander Pope titled 'Eloisa to Abélard.' It's meant to be a letter from a woman in the thirteenth century to the priest she fell in love with. When they were caught, they were separated, and the church punished him with castration and cast him out."

I clench my thighs. Is she threatening to cut my nuts off? "What has that got to do with me?"

She laughs wryly to herself. "Your father *loved* that poem. He was such a romantic—he believed in second chances and clean slates. I think before he died he believed he'd have one with you all. I tried to give him that. Now I see that there is no clean slate when you break things beyond repair. There's only whatever you can cobble together. And people will always be people. I can't expect you to be something you're not."

I run my hands over my face to stifle a scream. "What are you talking about?" *And can I fucking sit down?* The way she's talking is making me feel like my legs might not hold me. "Are you saying my father left us?"

"Yes, for another woman. For love. But he didn't just leave us, he walked away from Wilde World, too."

I don't give a shit what she says, I sit. I drop my head into my hands and try to make sense of what she's saying.

"Yes, just months later when we got word that he was missing and presumed dead, we did what we thought was best for the company, and the family. We rewrote that little blip in his history. Preserved his name and built a brand using his memory."

"You make it sound like nothing," I say, incredulous.

"It wasn't nothing, Tyson. But I'd already lost my husband, I wasn't going to lose everything I'd worked for, too."

"I see" is all I can manage.

"You're so much like your father. A romantic. I know you want to succeed me one day, but I don't think you're made for it."

I stand up again. Her words are like an astringent on my nerves and my worry. "Of course I was made for it. Just like he was."

"He wasn't. I'm not saying you can't be successful, Tyson. But the reason I'm alone isn't because I'm not interested in a life partner. Yes, I got married and had children...but I also believed in the vision your father had for this company. So I've given my life to it because that's what it takes. I'm built for it. "

"So am I."

"If you want me to believe that, you're going to have to do better than what you did last week. You put your feelings first, and look what it's cost you." I flinch at the way she characterized it. "Your rightful place."

I've heard people talk about out-of-body experiences, but I've never understood until this moment.

As my mother explains how the team I built this year will be redistributed to new roles and how my promotion will be deferred for a year, I feel like I'm watching it rather than experiencing it. My mother's lack of emotion is a stark contrast to the cyclone of emotions ripping across my face as her words sink in. But all I feel is a rush of adrenaline from the challenge she's laying at my feet. My nickname in school was The Daredevil. Tell me I can't, I'll show you why you should never underestimate me.

Being raised in the shadow of great people might have made an ordinary man insecure. But I'm no ordinary man. I've gone from runt to top dog once, and I can do it again. I've earned the right to the name. And if she thinks she can take it from me, she has another think coming.

1

I Dare You
Tyson
Ten Years Later

"You're not still thinking about moving to Paris, are you?" my older brother Remi's question breaks a very comfortable silence we've been sharing on his back porch.

I roll my head in his direction and let out a long-suffering sigh. "I was in a good mood, man, can you not ruin it with talk about that?"

"I know you decided to apply after you didn't get the promotion. But I'm just saying, after Mom's announcement tonight—"

I hold my hand up to stop him. "Please, don't say another word."

"Merry Christmas, bro." Remi's heavy hand comes down on my shoulder in a good-natured slap.

Surprised, I glance at my watch. "Oh shit, it's after midnight."

"And that is way past my bedtime." With a weary sigh, he hoists himself to his feet and yawns.

"Marriage is making you soft, man," I tease him, but my chuckle is cut off with a yawn of my own.

"But I can still kick your ass." He grins down at me. "And I've got a fine woman, who I get to keep all to myself, waiting up for me because she can't fall asleep if I'm not there."

I pick up the sweating tumbler from the table next to my chair and swirl the remaining slivers of ice at the bottom. "I hope you think it's worth it when you wake up at the crack of dawn tomorrow to put on that stupid suit and play Santa for a bunch of farting, ungrateful kids for two hours."

"Oh, I'd wear it every day for a year if it meant I could have her."

I shake my head in dismay. "How the mighty have fallen," I quip.

He chuckles. "I can't wait for it to happen to you."

I snort a laugh. "Don't hold your breath. I've got miles to go before I'm ready to think about that."

"And the best part is, you'll never see it coming."

"I've got a plan. If I can't see it, it can't see me." I throw back the watered-down whiskey and ice and reach for the snifter of liquor.

He snatches it out of my way. "That's the last thing you need, lightweight." With a warning glance, he walks back into the house, leaving me alone with my empty glass and heavy thoughts.

And they wonder why I want to move. They can't stop seeing the scrawny runt I was and reminding me that no matter how old I get, they'll never believe that I can take care of myself, much less the family's legacy.

I glance around the dark spot-lit backyard of my brother's house. It's big enough for a pool and a patio and has a section that I know will eventually play host to a swing set or treehouse.

But it's a far cry from the palatial grounds and manicured lawns of the mansion we grew up in. It's certainly not what anyone would expect for the man who is the head of one of the richest families in the country. But just like the life, career, and wife Remi chose, it fits him.

I envy him that—knowing what he wants, being sure about where he belongs.

I used to think I knew exactly where my life was going. So much so, that I've spent the ten years since the slip-up with Kayleigh busting my ass to prove that I was fit to lead.

But it wasn't enough. A few months ago, my mother passed me up for the job I'd spent my whole life preparing for, despite the fact that I was more than qualified for it. I went from being the heir apparent to lead at Wilde World—a role I'd always thought of as my destiny—to facing the possibility that it might not happen.

The bonds of my relationship with my mother have gone from strained to threadbare. She likes to say everything changed in the blink of an eye, but the truth is, nothing changed at all. She just saw something of my father in me that she hated, and she's been making me pay for his sins ever since.

But I'm done letting her.

I walk over to the railing of the wraparound porch and stare out into the night, rolling my neck to loosen the knots that always form when I think about my fucked-up family.

This job I've been pursuing in Paris would give me a chance to breathe and see who I can be without them. And then tonight, my mother makes her announcement. That not only does she have a man— she's moving her offices to London to be close to him. I'm happy for her, but it's not exactly the distance I was hoping for.

A door on the other end of the verandah opens, and a woman steps through it, but she's too shadowed for me to see who it is.

"It doesn't matter what you say, I'm done." It's Dina, Wilde World's newest star employee and current president of the Tyson Wilde Haters Association. The membership is comprised of disgruntled one-night stands, athletic rivals, and guys I've fucked up for disrespecting my sister.

Dina isn't any of those things, so I don't know why she acts like I've got cooties, but it's been a lot of fun to tease her about it.

Not that I don't wish I could convince her differently. Not only is she fucking beautiful. I mean, even dressed in those boring work clothes she wears, she made my *"seen everything at least once"* eyes do a double take the first time I saw her.

She's also one of the smartest, most determined, and funniest people I've ever met. It's a good thing I'm so focused on my career because if I wasn't, Dina Lu is just the kind of woman who could make me take my eyes off the ball. Not that she's interested in me that way.

"Sign the papers, or a judge will do it for you," she snarls into the phone.

Aware that if she knew I was here she wouldn't be speaking so freely, I clear my throat loudly.

"Shit. I have to go." The light from the phone dies, and she calls out, "Is someone there?"

I don't respond right away. Not when I have the chance to look at her without receiving one of her death glares. The dress she's wearing would look simple and plain on anyone else, but on her body it can't be anything but sexy.

It's the first time in the year since she started working for us that I've seen her in anything but the terrible clothes she wears at the office. They do a near criminal disservice to her classic Coke bottle figure.

The makeup she's wearing makes her deeply slanted, wide-set

brown eyes look sultry and even more alluring than they do when she's barefaced. And instead of the tightly tamed bun she forces her large mane of curls into, tonight her hair falls in waves that skim her bare shoulders. My fingers dance at my side, itching to know if her skin is as soft as it looks.

"Who's there?" she repeats in a more forceful tone.

"Your walking wet dream," I quip as I step into the light that's spilling through the window between us.

She crosses her arms over her ample chest and gives me a withering frown. "I should have known that on a hellish night like this, I'd bump into the very devil himself."

I laugh, amused by her vexation. "I don't know why you put so much energy into pretending to dislike me."

"And I don't know why you're following me. Every time I turn around, there you are."

I laugh again, this time longer and louder. "I'm not following you. You, on the other hand, are clearly obsessed with me."

She rolls her eyes. "The only thing bigger than your ego—"

"Is my dick," I finish for her.

"Is your lack of *tact*," she says primly.

"And—my bank account," I add with a wink.

She scoffs. "You are so sad. You think money and your dick are all you have to give."

"They're all I *want* to give," I correct her.

"Also, *sad*."

"From what I just heard, seems like you gave more, and it didn't turn out too well for you. Now, who's sad and who's *right*?"

To my surprise, she doesn't shoot back a snappy retort. Instead, her lower lip trembles, and her shoulders slump. She turns forlorn eyes in my direction. "You're right. I'm sad *and* wrong. Love is for dummies." She covers her face with both hands, drops right into my lap, and starts to cry.

I know she's been going through a tough divorce, but I've never seen her anything other than energetic, snarky, or hyper focused at work. I don't know what to do with an emotional crying Dina. So I do what I'd want if I was feeling bad enough to cry in front of someone. I wrap an arm around her and run a soothing hand over her back. She presses her face into my shoulder, and her hair tickles my cheek and my neck. It smells like fruit, and I want to bury my face in it.

She pulls away and saves me from embarrassing myself. "I'm sorry I cried all over you. I'm fine," she says in a weepy, small voice.

I push her hair back from her face and smile. "It's okay to cry. Even the strongest people need a soft place to land every once in a while."

"It's the alcohol, I had too much," she protests.

"I didn't have enough," I confess with a wry smile.

She pats my chest as if to console me. "Well, I'm glad because if you did, who would carry me upstairs to bed?"

"This house doesn't have stairs," I remind her with a laugh.

"Then it's your lucky day. This ass is as heavy as it looks." She smiles and drops her head back onto my shoulder and closes her eyes.

"Are you asleep?" I ask after a full minute of listening to her deep breathing.

"No, I'm smelling you."

My burst of surprised laughter jostles us both. "Smelling me?"

"Mmm-hmm, I knew you'd smell this good."

"You've thought about the way I smell?" I ask, even though I shouldn't.

"Oh, yeah, but it's much better than my imagination." She presses the cold tip of her nose into my neck and sniffs loudly. "I'm mad I waited so long to do this," she says.

"How long have you been waiting?"

She lifts her head from my shirt. Her eyes are still wet but aren't sad as she looks up into my face with a light in her eyes that I've never seen before. "Since the first time I saw you."

"You're drunk. You don't mean it." I laugh, but it's thin and false. The air around us seems to thicken, and my eyes are riveted to that luscious, sweet, hot mouth of hers.

"You know I do. And I know you want me, too. I've seen the way you watch me."

Oh, do I ever, but I can't encourage her. "We work together, so it hasn't crossed my mind."

Her face transforms with a dangerously knowing smile, and she leans toward me. Her pretty dark-red lips part, and her tongue darts out to lick them. The sight of the glistening pink flesh does *things* to my dick.

"Hasn't it?" she murmurs.

I want to kiss her. So badly. But I know better. And in the morning, she'll regret this. So I shake my head. "No."

"You are a liar," she whispers and then without warning presses her lips to mine.

I'm not prepared for this full-frontal assault, and when her tongue slides over my top lip, I can't hold back the groan that her honeypot of a mouth elicits. She tastes so good, and I want to drown in her sweetness.

She shifts in my lap so she's straddling me, and my hands go into autopilot and cup her voluptuous ass to draw her heat closer to mine.

I sink my teeth into her plump bottom lip and suck it into my mouth. With a whimper that makes my dick jump, her hands glide up my shoulders to cup the back of my neck.

She whimpers again, and the sound triggers a frenzy in me. My mind shouts, "more" over and over until I don't remember my own name.

I cup her breast and knead it until her nipple furls tightly against my palm. Her hips writhe against my thighs, and I break our kiss, panting to catch my breath. "I want to suck your nipples." I drag my lips down her creamy neck, and the way she smells is making me crazy.

"Yes, they're aching so badly. I want you to," she pants in my ear, and I lower my head and bite her nipple through the fabric of her dress. Her head falls back, and I suck hard, desperate to get as much of her in my mouth as possible.

Fuck this dress she's wearing, I want to taste her. I lift up off the chair and turn us so she's seated and kneel in front of her.

I shove her dress up, push her panties to the side, and almost expire on the spot. "Your pussy smells so fucking good."

"Oh, wait until you taste it," she sighs, and her hands slip in my hair.

I dip my tongue and take a slow, greedy lick before I bury my face in between her thighs and start to eat her in earnest. God, I'm drunk on her after just few licks, and I want to make her come so badly. I want to see the look on her face when she falls apart with my name on her lips.

But before I can make that happen, the light on the porch comes on. I jump up and back away from her. Remi is standing in the window, arms crossed over his chest, watching me with a look of stern disapproval on his face before he turns and heads back into the house.

Shit. That is the last fucking thing I need.

"Who's there?" Dina asks as she comes to stand next to me, tugging her dress down.

"It was just Remi. He's gone," I tell her. But I don't sit. What the hell was I thinking?

"Whew," she says as she sits back down and grabs my hand. Her lips, still glistening from our kiss, tip up at the corners. "Now, where were we?"

"Stopping, Dina. You're drunk. You should just go to bed."

"Only if you come with me."

I laugh and shake my head, but my heart is racing. I want to go with her, but I know why Remi was looking at me like that. I know better than to let the lines of work and pleasure get blurred again. "Just be grateful I know you deserve better than what I have to offer. Otherwise, you'd be in real trouble."

"I don't want better than what you have to offer. I want you to kiss me again."

I laugh and pull her to her feet. "You're crazy."

She scoffs. "So you're telling me that kiss didn't fry your circuits?"

"I've had better," I lie again.

She laughs and shakes her head. "Maybe it's for the best. It would be terrible to fall for you." She stands toe-to-toe with me and gazes up into my eyes, all humor gone from her expression. "I want my fairy tale next or nothing at all. No regrets on the amazing head, but it will never happen again. So Merry Christmas. I'm gonna go to bed now." Then she turns on her pretty little heel and walks away.

I sit in the chair she just vacated, and it's still warm from our bodies. So I get up. I don't want to remember how good that felt. Drunk or not, I don't trust myself not to seek her out again tonight. And that would be asking for all sorts of trouble.

Romance, love, relationships—they are my axis of evil. I haven't dated since that debacle ten years ago. And as a rule, I don't fuck women I work with or socialize with. Dina more than checks both of those boxes.

Regan inviting her to spend Christmas Eve with us is a big deal. They're more than just casual friends, she thinks of Dina as family. And over the course of a year of seeing her at our weekly family Friday night dinners, I do too.

Even if those things weren't true, I don't have time for a relationship. I've lost ground I need to make up and I need to focus.

Damn if I don't hate to do it though, because I like Dina Lu. A lot. She looks me straight in the eye, she doesn't pretend or play coy. And after a lifetime of secrets and false faces, she's a breath of fresh air.

But I've got too much to figure out and can't consign myself to the same spiral of hell I've watched all my friends and family go through when love caught up with them.

We blurred a line tonight that needs redrawing right away. I've been served well by being unapologetically self-centered, ambitious, and unavailable. She wants a fairy tale, and I'm not anything close to Prince Charming.

All I can give her is the one thing we *both* need.

Distance.

This job in Paris will do that. And until then, I'll stay away from her. The sooner I get out of Rivers Wilde, the better for both of us.

2

Hunting Her Daredevil
Dina
Three Months Later

Go get your man, D. Call me when you get home

The text from my best friend, Beth pops up on my phone, and the hand I have poised to swipe more mascara starts to tremble.

There have been ninety-one sunsets since Christmas Eve, but the intensity of the nervous anticipation that swells in my chest makes it feel like I'm back on that porch with Tyson.

I'd had too much to drink, but I wasn't really drunk. The contentious conversation with my soon to be ex-husband rubbed salt in a raw wound, and I just really needed some comfort.

I didn't expect those tears. But it felt so good to lean on Tyson. And to have him willingly take some of the weight for me.

I'd been crushing on him from the minute I walked smack dab into him on my first day of work. But I didn't ever expect that we'd be friends. Tyson was as precise and uncompromising as the crisp, snow-white dress shirts with monogrammed gold cufflinks he wore every single day. He wore these immaculately knotted ties that were always the same color as his expensive suits, and he never smiled. Not at anyone. He was a task master, known for impatience, intensity, and success. We never spoke, and as far as I knew, he'd never even glanced in my direction.

Not that I expected him to.

So it was only after his sister and I became friends, and she invited me to join their Friday night family dinners that I realized he had two personas. The man he is outside the office was a daredevil, a prankster who meddled in his siblings' love lives and spoiled his nieces and nephews rotten. He was the most charming flirt, and I caught the appreciative glances he'd send my way every so often. I let him tease me. He let me bust his balls. Our Friday night dinner crew called us frenemies who flirted. But until I dropped myself into his lap on Christmas Eve, we'd never, ever actually touched.

He is the living, breathing definition of gorgeous. His six-foot frame is a muscular masterpiece covered in smooth caramel-colored skin. His eyes are wide and dark as a starless night, heavy-lidded, thickly lashed, and dreamy. The bold curve of his cheekbones and his cleanly shaven strong jaw beg to be stroked. And his broad, lush mouth tasted like heaven when we finally kissed.

God, that *kiss*. I haven't been able sleep for replaying the memories of what his dark head looked like buried between my thighs.

On Christmas morning, I'd woken up to help Remi's wife, Kal, prep for lunch. But I'd chickened out of staying to eat. I was glad he'd had better sense than me, but I couldn't face him.

At that point, my divorce drama was almost over, I finally had a good job, and I didn't want to let myself get distracted.

Turns out I didn't need to worry about that. I started skipping the standing Friday night dinners we had at Regan's house to spend some time with my dad.

I kept telling myself what I told Tyson that night—leaving each other alone was for the best. I busied myself with helping my dad with a passion project and holding my best friend's hand through some of the darkest days of her life. I gave Tyson the wide berth he was giving me, too.

And my new job on the competitive intelligence team at Wilde kept me busy.

I was born with an uncanny ability to read people. It made my teachers, friends, even my parents uncomfortable at times. I'm not a mind reader, so I could never say why, but I could sense when someone liked me or didn't. Whether they were lying or not. And I was never wrong. As an adult, I make a living hunting down the truth and protecting people from liars. My mother used to call me a human lie detector.

Human lie detector my *ass*. I didn't see the liar in the mirror until the lie blew up in my face.

Two weeks ago, I sat watching Beth being serenaded by the love of her life and realized that despite the crushing disappointment of my failed marriage, I wanted a moment like that, too. My fairy tale didn't have a white knight who whisked in to take me away, but a man who was strong enough to handle me.

And who was secure enough to tell the whole world that I was the most important person in his life. Not on a stage in front of the whole world like what happened to Beth—I mean, that would be mortifying—but in ways that say I matter. I needed that.

And as that realization sank in, all I could think about was Tyson and the kiss that made me burn for more.

I wanted to finish crying on his shoulder and talk to him about his dad, tell him about my mom. I wanted to give him a soft place to land, too.

I got back from that visit with Beth determined to find Tyson and tell him all of that. But like the hero in every Greek tragedy I read in high school, by the time I realized my fatal flaw, it was too little, too late.

That same day, I saw the announcement about his posting to Paris. His going away party was tonight, and even as visions of disastrous scenarios that all ended with a very public rejection swam in my head, I said I'd be there. I wanted at least to say goodbye. And maybe, if I hadn't blown it, say more.

This morning, I went to Helena's on Richmond to get waxed and lady-scaped. I called in a favor from a former client who works at Leon Nails and got my feet done. Then I spent the rest of the day washing, twisting, and drying my hair. I even bought a new dress.

By the time Regan called to say she was on her way to pick me up, I was a bundle of tightly drawn nerves, but determined to see it through.

Until she told me her mother was going to be there, too.

I can count on one hand the number of people I live my life in awe of. And long before I knew her children or worked for the company she built, Tina Wilde has been one of them.

I might be able to stomach making a fool out of myself in front of Tyson. After all, he'll be gone tomorrow, and I won't have to bear the humiliation of seeing him every day.

But the thought of his mother being witness to it proved too much to bear. So I told Regan I wasn't feeling well and asked her to make my apologies.

I check the time. It's almost midnight. He's sure to be home by now. I can go, say my piece, and leave.

I eye the half-finished bottle of Riesling on my counter with disgust. I shouldn't have had so much to drink. I don't trust my tipsy self's judgment when it comes to this man. What if this is all just liquid courage I'll regret, deeply, in the morning?

Torn and aware of my closing window of opportunity, I call my best friend Beth—again.

"So what's the verdict? Are you going?" she asks as soon as she answers.

"I still don't know that I should," I admit. "I mean, he didn't even tell me he was leaving." On a pained groan, I flop back onto my bed and stare at my ceiling.

"Dina, come on," Beth cajoles. "You're friends with his sister, you work in the same place. Maybe he just assumed you knew?"

I scoff. "That man doesn't *assume* anything."

"He's human, Dina. We *all* make assumptions. You should go. You're going to regret not saying goodbye."

"Maybe, but I'll regret it even more if he laughs in my face. Or even worse, what if he's not alone?" My stomach lurches at the thought of it.

"Listen, babe. I know you're scared to be vulnerable, but if you're this tied in knots, you should go talk to him. No matter what he says, at least you'll know where he stands. You guys have been dancing around this thing for a while now. And you said it yourself, you haven't exactly been forthright with him. Maybe if you open up, it will help him do the same."

"Oh, I doubt that." My stomach twists when I think about how abruptly and completely he disappeared from my life after our encounter on the porch on Christmas Eve.

"D, hold on," Beth exclaims, and then in the next breath she says, "Sorry, babe, it's Carter. We're leaving tomorrow, and everything is a mess. Hold on just a sec." She clicks over before I can tell her not to worry about it. I'm tired of talking about Tyson.

Less than ten seconds pass before she clicks back. "D—"

"I know. You've got to go."

"Sorry, my passport isn't here. And—"

"No, don't explain. I understand. Go."

"I hate leaving you alone right now."

"I'm fine. Go be happy globe-trotting with your famous, gorgeous boyfriend, and send me all the details so I can live vicariously through you."

After we hang up, I walk to my dresser and open the small pink jewelry box I keep there. It was a gift from my mother on my twelfth birthday, and the last thing she gave me before she died. Almost twenty years later, the small box's dusky exterior is worn, the music box inside is broken, and the spinning ballerina's glossy ceramic finish is chipped. But the words on the note she wrote me, the one I still reach for in moments when I'm afraid, are just as powerful.

"People will look at you and see only that you are small. Or that you look different. But like this ballerina, you are more flexible and resilient than you appear. If you work hard, are honest and brave, you'll find that you are capable of pivots, leaps and spins that will take you wherever you want to go. And when you feel like you can't take one more step, that's only fear talking. The world and everything in it, is yours my miraculous girl. So, when you feel afraid, I hope you'll remember that and do it anyway."

I check the time again. It's almost midnight. If I'm going to do this, I have to do it now. I strip, put on the only matching set of underwear I own, and slip into my raincoat. I order an Uber to his place, slide on my single pair of high heels, and head out.

On the way over, I'm riddled with doubt for most of the ride. What am I even going to say? What if he's not home? Or not alone? I shake that thought loose. I spent ten years in a marriage that lasted nine years too long. I'm done putting my happiness on hold. If he rejects me, it won't kill me. But wondering if he was the one I let get away might.

As the car pulls off the busy, commercial-lined aorta of Houston, Westheimer Road, and onto the leafy tree-lined street of Wildewood Parkway, I roll the window down and take a deep breath. The transition in environments is so drastic, it's almost like driving through a portal to another world. And it never fails to relax me. There's just *something* about this stretch of road that feels like coming in out of the cold. Rivers Wilde isn't *really* a small town, because it sits right in the heart of the nation's fourth largest city. Which in the eyes of a girl who grew up in a small town makes it something even better. Because it gives you the escape from the city, the close-knit community, the cluster of small businesses that double as watering holes. But it's also welcoming of outsiders and thrives on its diverse population of residents.

The enclave is subdivided into two residential sections: The Oaks, a community of single-family homes that range in size from bungalows to full-on mansions, is an idyllic sprawl of manicured lawns, wide streets canopied by fragrant magnolia trees, and dotted with *Children Playing* signs every few hundred feet.

The Ivy, a cluster of towering chrome and glass high-rises, was designed to cater to the lifestyles of singles or married without children couples. It has twenty-four-hour restaurants and exercise facilities. Several coffee shops with plenty of seating, and free Wi-Fi. You can pick up your dry cleaning, go to the bank, and mail a package without ever leaving the complex. And when you feel like socializing, Rivers Wilde's main street is less than a ten-minute walk away and is brimming with world class restaurants and bars. I plan on moving in as soon as the lease at my current place was up.

"Hello? We're here." My driver's raised voice shakes me out of my mental meander.

"Sorry, thanks." I give him an apologetic smile that he returns and climb out.

My doubt comes surging back, but I don't break stride as I cross the luxurious, terrazzo-tiled lobby toward the bank of elevators. The doors open as I approach, and I hesitate a beat. Do I really want to do this?

Yes. He's *leaving*. I take a deep breath, step on, and press the button for the 20th floor. My heart is beating a nervous galloping rhythm when I arrive at his floor, and by the time I reach the door of his unit, I'm dizzy with nervous energy and trepidation.

The door flies open right before I knock, and I jump back with a yelp of surprise. Tyson's assistant, a Sudanese bombshell who used to model before she came to work for him, stops short in front of me, her purse on her shoulder and her keys in her hand. Her brow furrows as she looks me over. "Can I help you?"

I've only met her a few times, but clearly I didn't make the impression on her that she made on me because she's acting like she's never seen me before. "Hi, Fatima. I work at Wilde World. My name is Dina," I add when her frown only deepens.

She leans away, scans me from head to toe, and then her eyes widen in recognition. "Wait, oh my God." She laughs and shakes her head. "I just didn't recognize you without the...black clothes. You're The Hunter."

I laughed the first time my assistant told me that's what people called me because of my all black all the time wardrobe. "Uh—yeah. I guess so. That's me."

She grimaces in apology. "Sorry, you don't really look like a hunter. It's just you know you like hunt down stuff? And you wear all black…"

"Yes. I know, but thanks." I give her a tight smile and glance over her shoulder into the apartment.

"Wait, are you here for …*Mr. Wilde?*" The disbelief in her voice and the way her eyebrows disappear into her hairline as she takes in my cliché as fuck bootycall getup makes knots of dread form in my gut. The last thing I need is gossip around the office about this.

I force myself to smile. "I missed his party earlier, was in the area, and thought I'd stop in to say goodbye. I didn't realize he had company."

"I'm not company, I work for him. Come on in." She doesn't wait for me to answer before she disappears back inside.

I hesitate. This was a bad idea, but if I leave now he'll know I was here. Besides, I didn't come this far to *only* come this far. So I pull my big girl panties up and step inside the devil's lair.

"Sorry, there's nowhere to sit but on the boxes. I'll go tell him you're here." She saunters down the hallway and sticks her head into an open door. "Mr. Wilde, you have company," she yells, and then comes back to the living room to slip her shoes on. "He's in the shower, so it'll be a minute. I'm going to pick up some food from Frenchy's. Do you want anything?"

"No, I'm good," I reply absently as I make a one hundred and eighty degree turn around the room. I've never been here before. I used to wonder what side of his personality would win out when it came to decorating the devil's lair. Would it be the monochromatic, expensive, look but don't touch style of Tyson at work? Or the colorful, relaxed, but intentional style of the Tyson he is in private? Or, would I discover that, he's everything I've ever wanted in a man—and a little bit of both?

I trap the flutter happiness before it disappears and stow it away for later.

It would be a fool's errand to anchor such heavy hopes on the fragile foundation of we have. And I'm no fool.

I know that this is more about the idea of him than anything else. *But what an idea it is.*

His door opens, and I get ready to throw this Hail Mary. I think he's worth it. I hope like hell he proves me right.

3

Beautiful Liar
Tyson

I heard Fatima shout over the shower's thundering spray, but couldn't make out what she said. She came over to go through my list for the movers. I'll be gone when they come to get my stuff, and she's the only person I trust to make sure nothing important gets left behind.

I didn't eat a thing at the party Regan threw, and I hope Fatima's already made that food run.

This move happened so fast, I barely had time to finish packing before it was time to leave. I throw on the only pair of jeans and one of the T-shirts I haven't packed and walk out to the living room. "Did you say someone was here?" I call down the hall.

"It's the Hunter," she calls back. I stop mid-step. That wasn't Fatima's voice. It *sounded* like her…but it couldn't be. "Dina?" I ask, rounding the corner slowly. I'm surprised she's here. I thought we'd come to a tacit agreement to keep our distance from each other. I was disappointed and relieved when she wasn't at my party tonight and had resigned myself to not seeing her again before I left.

"Oh, hey, Tyson," she drawls and gives a wave like it's perfectly normal for her to be in my house.

I cross my arms over my chest and raise a skeptical brow at her far too casual hello. "What are you doing here?"

She swallows audibly and tightens her belt around her waist. "I was in the neighborhood and thought I'd come to say goodbye since you were clearly not going to."

Annoyed, I narrow my eyes and frown at her. "You didn't come to my going away party, and you haven't spoken to me in three months. I figured *that* was goodbye."

Her shoulders stiffen, and that stubborn chin of hers tilts up. "I thought *you* weren't speaking to me, and I had a lot going on."

"Well, so did I. And like you said, it was better we didn't do anything we'd regret."

"I thought we were friends. I read about your new job in a corporate announcement. You didn't say a word."

"I didn't think you would care. I thought you'd be glad I was going, in fact."

She stares at me in surprise. Opens her mouth and then closes it again. "Tyson, come on. Really?" she finally says, exasperation marring her smooth brow.

That's what I've been telling myself. Remi chewed my ear off Christmas morning about what he'd almost walked in on. But he didn't need to. The complete loss of control I showed out on that porch shook me.

I was attracted to her, yes. But I didn't make promises I couldn't keep. And I knew that sober, sagacious Dina would know that I wasn't the man who could give her the fairy tale she wanted.

I run my eyes over her. She's wearing a raincoat on a very warm and dry March evening. I hate that I'm not going to get to find out whether she's wearing anything underneath it or not. "It doesn't matter now. I'm leaving tomorrow."

She flinches like I slapped her and drops her eyes to the ground. "I shouldn't have come." Her voice trembles, and something in my chest twists painfully.

The only thing harder than the work it takes to reach the goals I set are the things I've had to give up along the way. I can't afford to fuck this opportunity up, and it's not fair to Dina to ask her for something I can't give her in return.

She wipes her hands over her cheeks and sniffles.

"Don't cry. I don't want to make you sad."

Her gaze snaps up to meet mine, and her eyes glitter with indignation. "Alcohol makes me cry. I'm not sad."

"You're such a bad liar, Dina."

"And you're a little too good at it, Tyson."

I cup her face, and her cheeks are hot underneath my cool palms. I stroke her cheekbones with the pads of my thumbs, and her eyes close on a sigh that I recognize as a sound of the same relief I feel.

It's been so long since I touched her. She's so soft, and I want her so much.

Against my better judgment and pulled by forces I can't control, I run the tip of my nose down the slope of hers. "Let me give you something you can feel the truth of," I whisper.

Her exhaled breath kisses my lips right before my mouth covers hers.

She opens for me, and her hands grasp either side of my waist as she starts to kiss me back.

Her soft, pliant lips taste of delicious things I'll never get tired of—sweet, heat, opportunity, desire, ambition.

Her tongue teases mine, my lips suck, my teeth tug, and for a few frantic, fevered moments I let myself imagine this could be different. But that only makes the dread and regret I'm feeling about what I have to do even more acute.

I break our kiss and step away. "We shouldn't do that again. It's for your own good. I promise."

Her eyes narrow in disgust, and she looks me up and down. "Oh, for God's sake stop acting like this is to spare me. I'm a grownup, Tyson. I'm not wearing rose colored glasses. It's fine if you don't want me or you're not ready. But don't insult me with this patronizing you know best bullshit."

"It's not bullshit. And it *is* best."

One corner of her mouth tips down in a disdainful frown. "You don't know what's *best* for me. You're trying to protect *yourself* from whatever you think is going to happen if you admit you want more than your job. Which is fine. But you should be honest with me."

She hits the bullseye and strips me to the bone with that too close to home truth. I've said too much. She sees too much. She makes me weak in ways I can't afford to be. The throb in my chest grows stronger every second she stands here. A lifetime of practice makes it easy to build a wall around it. All I need to do is to recall that conversation I overheard. She feels this way now, but one day, she'll get tired of playing second fiddle and leave. This has to stop here.

I step away from her and walk to the door. "I tried honesty that night. I told you it wasn't a good idea. I tried keeping my distance. And yet here you are. You should learn to take no for an answer. And I think you should go." Each word is a brick of lies in that wall I'm building. And by the time I reach the door, my nerves are settled again, and I turn to face her.

Her jaw has dropped, and her eyes bulge with affront as she stalks toward me. "As *if*. You can pretend you feel nothing. But take it from me, you'll be sorry you didn't at least try. I hope your job and Paris and all the random strangers you'd rather have sex with than me make you happy, you jerk." She casts me one long, searing look and then walks out of my life.

I'm sitting in the middle of my bare living room, stewing in annoyance and regret when Fatima walks back in almost an hour later.

"I had to drive all the way to the Frenchy's near TSU to get this. You're lucky I didn't eat it all on my way back." She waves the fragrant plastic bag full of the famous Frenchy's fried chicken. I don't have to the heart to tell her I'm not interested in eating anymore. She walks into the living room and looks around the apartment. "She left?" she asks.

"Yes."

"So…you and her?"

"Don't ask."

When she doesn't say anything and doesn't move, I look up. She's watching me with a look of wonder on her face.

"What?" I snap irritably and get to my feet.

"Are you in love with the Hunter chick?"

I give her a warning look. "Her name is Dina. I'm not in love with her, and I'm trusting that her visit will stay between us."

She lowers her eyes to the ground, and I am instantly sorry for my tone and my words. Fatima has been with me since I started at Wilde, and she's the only person on my staff I'm taking with me to Paris. I trust her, and I like her. But she's already seen and heard more than I'm comfortable with. I keep work and personal separate.

"You know that without even having to ask. Are you okay, Mr. Wilde?"

"I'm fine."

Whether it's because she believes me or because she's afraid to push any harder, I'm not sure, but she drops it. "You hungry? I got the food," she calls over her shoulder as she moves back down the hall.

"Yeah, I'm coming." I join her in the kitchen and take the plate she hands me.

"Add this to the list of things I'm going to miss in Paris," she says around a mouthful of fried chicken when I join her in the bedroom to pack things up.

"Yeah, I guess."

"What are you going miss about Houston?"

Dina. Her name comes, unbidden and unwelcome. I banish it. "Not a damn thing."

4

Dream Come True
Dina
One Year Later

I stand in front of the wide oak doors that lead to the inner sanctum of Tina Wilde's private office. Trepidation stills the hand I raise to knock on it in mid-air. Her email summoning me here this morning was terse and urgent. I'm prepared for the worst—termination for insubordination—as my boss threatened in his email last week.

I stuck my neck out knowing this could happen, but I didn't actually think it would. I should have kept my mouth shut. But I can't seem to learn that lesson.

I scrutinize the corners of the doorway to her office. My trained eyes don't see the telltale signs of the surveillance cameras she had installed there a few days ago, but I know they're there. Even though that recommendation is the domino that started the chain of events that led me to this moment, I can't help but smile.

"When you're done preening, please come in," the head honcho herself calls, the impatience in her voice loud and clear through the door as I push it open and stride into her large window-lined corner office.

The apology on the tip of my tongue is stilled by the heart-stopping view. London spreads out before me like a living postcard. The mighty River Thames winds through the city as far as my eye can see. Spanned by the medieval London Bridge on one end, its banks are dotted, in equal measure, with centuries old structures and modern buildings made of glass and steel. They're a testament to the city's commitment to its history and its willingness to adapt in order to maintain its global dominance as one of the world's leading financial and cultural centers. I wish I had time to explore.

"Hello Dina, nice to see you, too."

At her sardonic comment, I wince and turn to face her. "I'm so sorry, Mrs. Wilde. Hello. It's very nice to see you." I hope the surprise I feel at her appearance doesn't show on my face and relax when she smiles. "It's okay. It's an incredible view, and you're allowed an awestruck moment." She gestures at the small sitting area in front of the windows. "Have a seat, we'll have our meeting there. I just need to finish sending this email and I'll be right with you."

I nod and sit. I can't help nestling against the soft buttery leather of the huge, tufted armchair. But only for a second. I don't relax and enjoy the view.

Instead, I study the woman who built the food service and retail empire that employs a quarter of a million people around the globe and marvel that I'm sitting in her office.

"Okay, all done," she announces and presses a button on her desk. "Emily, please order a pot of tea for my meeting. Herbal tea, please."

"Yes, ma'am" comes the response of her brisk, efficient assistant who must have the hardest job of anyone in this company but makes it look like a piece of cake.

She sits back in her chair and chuckles to herself. "The first time I ordered herbal tea, she was horrified." She laughs again. "I tried to do as the Romans and all that, but the caffeine is hell on my skin and makes my heart race even faster than it already does. Are you ready?"

She rises from her high-backed, throne-like chair and makes her way across the room to join me by the window. Her walk is looser. She used to move like an army general in long, ground-eating strides. Now she struts, her hips loose and swaying just a little.

The perfectly contoured foundation and matte berry-colored lipstick she normally wears have been replaced with softer highlights and nude lip gloss. I suspect the man she moved here to be with, an actor named Max Priest, is responsible for the loosening and lightening that's taken place since she moved here.

Not that I would dare mention it. She's nice to me when she sees me socially, but I wouldn't presume anything more than a professional relationship with her.

There's a light tap on her door before it opens and her assistant walks in, pushing a silver service cart topped with some pretty light blue and gold china and a lot more than tea—sandwiches, cookies, and fresh fruit are piled on a three-tiered stand.

"Thank you, Emily."

"Ma'am," Emily says by way of reply and then she leaves the room.

"Keep talking, I'll pour and serve."

"Okay…" I say and try to hide my astonishment at the sight of Tina Wilde serving *me*.

She places a cup onto a saucer and glances up at me. "Sugar or milk?"

"In my tea?" I ask quizzically.

"They drink it like we drink coffee. I really like it. How do you take your coffee?"

"Dark and sweet, please."

She pours some of the dark steaming liquid into the mug and then uses a small pair of silver tongs to drop a square cube of sugar into the cup and hands it to me.

"Thank you." I take it from her and lift it to my nose.

"I called you here to discuss your future at Wilde World."

My throat closes, and my heart starts to pound, and I set the cup down so I can clasp my trembling hands in my lap.

"I know the email was insubordinate and impulsive. I'm sorry I spoke so crassly."

She cocks her head to the side and purses her lips. "Are you saying that because Derrick has asked HR to put you on a performance plan?"

My stomach feels like a thousand goldfish are swimming in it. A PP, as they're known by, is just a CYA for the process of firing an employee.

"No. I'm not sorry I sent it. I'm sorry I copied Erin and sorry I used that kind of language."

She smiles faintly and nods but doesn't say anything as she looks at me. "I'm sorry to hear that. I like how remarkably unapologetic you were. Especially the line about Derrick being mediocre and the rest of us suffering for it. And not wanting to work for an organization where merit didn't matter and honesty was optional."

I squirm under her scrutiny and at how harsh my words sound repeated back to me. "I was angry. I know that one person doesn't represent the ethos of the entire company. And I wouldn't do anything to jeopardize my career here."

"I hope not because you're smart, you're efficient, and you're a very good leader. Your team in Houston respects and likes you—and that is a rare thing. I want to see you thrive. I'd hate to see you get in your own way by being impulsive and letting your emotions rule you."

Chastised, I nod. "It won't happen again. I apologized to Derrick yesterday and will apologize to Erin when I leave your office."

"There's no need for that. They've both been terminated this morning."

She opens her iPad and starts scrolling through it, and I'm glad she doesn't expect me to respond because I couldn't form a coherent thought if I tried.

Panicked and wildly confused by her announcement, I connect the dots of the sequence of events that brought me to London in the first place and try to reconcile them with what she just said.

"Because of my email?"

She snorts a laugh. "Of course not. But before I tell you, please sign this non-disclosure agreement. This is highly sensitive. I've received clearance from legal to share it with you, and only you. Revealing it will expose you, me, and the entire organization to legal action."

Stunned by the news and more than a little bit afraid of what I'm about to learn, I nod. "Okay, sure. I'll sign it."

She slides it across the small table. "I'm going to the powder room. Read it, and if you agree, sign it. We'll continue when I get back."

What in the world? They've *both* been fired? Erin is relatively new to the role of chief operations officer. She created this director of corporate intelligence role for Derrick, my boss, and they both just moved to London with Mrs. Wilde.

I hadn't been sad to see the back of him. He was underqualified and overconfident. When he asked me to be part of the team he was assembling to design the new security and privacy protocols for the London office, I expected to do most of the work.

I'd never been to London before that, and the idea of spending three weeks there, all expenses paid by someone else, was too good to pass up, so I didn't blink before I said yes.

At the end of my trip, we met to present our plan to Erin before she presented it to Mrs. Wilde, and I realized that every single one of the recommendations in the report were mine. And that the one I made about surveillance equipment in the office was incomplete. When I mentioned it, Derrick reprimanded me in front of the whole team and called my recommendation for cameras overkill.

After the meeting, Erin called me into her office. Derrick was waiting there with her, and he advised me because of my attempts to upstage him and insubordination, I was being given an official warning that would be placed in my permanent employee record.

Shocked and embarrassed, I apologized for my overreach and went back to Houston with my tail between my legs, praying I hadn't done fatal damage to what I had hoped was just the beginning of a long career at Wilde.

I was searching our team's shared drive and I scrolled past the finalized security plan for Mrs. Wilde's new office.

My sixth sense made me stop, go back, and open it. The plan that Derrick filed included all of my recommendations, including the cameras. And in the cover letter he wrote her, he'd taken credit for all of them.

I was so angry that I sent him an email calling him out for not only stealing my work, but for reprimanding me for something just because he hadn't thought of it first.

It's hard enough being a woman in a field where men are treated like James Bond and women like Miss Marple. And if he did it to me once, he'd do it again. I wanted to make sure at least he would know he couldn't get away with it. So I copied both Erin and Mrs. Wilde on the email.

Derrick didn't respond, but the next day, I got an email from Mrs. Wilde summoning me back to London for a meeting. I haven't slept more than a few hours since I got it.

I thought I was going to get fired, but it turns out I was completely off the mark.

I sign the NDA, slide it back to her side of the table, and wait impatiently for her return.

When she sits down again, she scans it, smiles, and proceeds to blow my mind.

"Derrick and Erin are a couple. They have been since I hired her. All of that is in direct contravention of our anti-fraternization policy. And while we don't allow couples to work together, we understand that these things happen and have a process for disclosure and separation of interests, so we don't have issues like this. They decided to hide their relationship, and she let it influence her in her decision to promote and move him here—at great expense to the company."

My jaw drops. "Wow."

She smiles grimly. "Indeed. I found this out a day before your email landed in my inbox. And I was reminded that when one door closes, another one always opens. All that to say, Derrick's role is now vacant and will be based in Houston again, as it should be. I'd like you to fill it."

My heart skips a beat, and I grasp my hands in my lap to hide their trembling. "Me? Really?"

She chuckles. "Don't look so surprised. Your resume isn't traditional, but I like your gumption and that you aren't afraid to speak truth to power. And you're very, very good at your job. I'm sure, after a few more years here, you'd be able to write your own ticket, but I hope you'll stay and grow with Wilde World. We all care about you, Dina, and think of you as family."

"I don't know what to say. Derrick is a director. I'm two levels lower than that."

"Yes, and you'll have a steep learning curve in this role, and a few men who will resent you going from being their peer to their superior. But I see a lot of potential in you, and I want to nurture it. And I think you are up to the challenge."

"Thank you so much." I take a sip of my tea to hide the wide grin of surprise on my face, even though I know my eyes show my elation. The job she's offering me is the kind of opportunity I didn't think would come my way for a long time. But just like that, it's here.

At the same time happiness tugs at the corners of my mouth, gratitude tugs at the strings of my heart.

Hearing Tina Wilde say she sees potential in me and cares about me is one of the biggest compliments I've ever received. And it's the closest thing to mothering I've had from anyone in a long time. Not that she's anything at all like my mother.

She's almost sixty, the same age my mother would have been if she was still alive. She has the same cocoa brown complexion, too. But that's where the similarities end.

My mother treated me like I was the center of her universe. Tina Wilde's brand of mothering is to remind everyone that the universe *has* no center.

But galaxies do—and she is the center of this one. The rest of us—her children, her company, her employees—are planets kept in rotation by her gravitational pull.

"I'm so honored, Mrs. Wilde, thank you."

"Don't thank me yet. Derrick and Erin had an assignment that they won't be able to see through, and I'll need you to fill his shoes."

"Okay." I nod, excited at the possibilities unfolding in my mind.

She glances at the iPad and then frowns. "I see you're scheduled to leave for Paris Friday. Do you have plans set in stone there already?"

"No." But my stomach drops. It's my birthday on Saturday. I planned a weekend in Paris when I realized I'd be in London so close to the date. It's the one place I've always wanted to visit but never got the chance. I thought after I got fired, it might be my last chance for a long time.

But I wouldn't dream of telling Mrs. Wilde that. She's giving me an opportunity most people would kill for. My job at Wilde World is the reason I can afford to go to Paris at all. It's also the reason, after my divorce turned my life to rubble, I'm able to dig out of the financial rut it put me in.

My sessions at Orange Theory, virtual therapist on The Difference, being able to fly to New York for a weekend to see my best friend Beth, sending my dad on his first trip to Vietnam in twenty years, and being able to meet the monthly obligations on *both* my student loans and my lawyer—all of that was made possible by my job. So yeah, it sucks to cancel my plans, but with the salary that Derrick's job comes with, a flight to Paris from Houston won't break the bank like it might now..

My smile is fully sincere when I respond. "What's the assignment?"

Her eyes narrow, and she leans back in surprise. "Dina, I don't want you to feel as though you have to lie to me. I know it's your birthday, and I imagine you planned something lovely in Paris. I'm asking if any of it is set in stone, not because I want you to cancel everything but because I want to see how we can work around it."

"Oh—well, I just didn't want to seem ungrateful. And truly, there's nothing I've planned that won't wait."

She nods. "I offered you this job because it took character and courage to write that email. Those are qualities you can't teach or put a price on. But candor is important. I know everyone is scared of me. And I know it will take some time for you to get used to working so closely with me. But you'll find that I'm not a dragon who rips the heads off the employees who disappoint me. I'm just a woman with a lot of responsibility and not a lot of time. I think time will do more to convince you of that than anything I can say."

I laugh, surprised at how good-natured she is about the nickname the staff uses behind her back. "Okay. And thank you. I'm thrilled you trust me to dive right in. I'll do my best, I promise."

She nods in approval. "Well, I'm glad. And even though I'm asking you to work this weekend, I hope that some parts of the assignment will feel like a bit of an upgrade."

I can't hide my relief. "Thank you for considering that."

"Of course. I'm an old dog, but I'm learning some new tricks. As you know, we're expanding in Europe. And our plans hinge on the purchase of smaller specialty food chains. We have our eye on Dupont. You're familiar with them?"

I nod. "Yes, they're a small London-based grocer that opened six locations in France last year. They expanded too quickly and are now looking for a buyout."

Surprise lifts both her brows. "Very good."

"I did the research for the brief Derrick presented."

"Of course, you did. So you know then, that there's a day of investor meetings in Fontainebleau on Saturday. Erin was going to go and make our presentation. Derrick was going to accompany her and do a little reconnaissance—and make sure there weren't any landmines that could blow up in our faces."

"And you want me to go with you instead?" I point at my chest.

She shakes her head. "I can't attend."

My jaw drops. "I'm flattered, but I don't think I'm any replacement for you or Erin."

She laughs. "I'm not asking you to. I want you to do the work Derrick was going to, but a little differently now that I'm slotting you into his place. You'll leave for Paris tonight. You'll have Thursday to get ready. On Friday you and Tyson will attend a social function with Mr. Dupont's son and self-proclaimed successor, George Jr. Saturday morning, you'll head out to Fontainebleau with Tyson and the rest of the attendees. The men will head into their meetings. Their partners are invited to spend the day at the spa and do some sight-seeing. Where are you staying?"

"I'm sorry. Did you...say *Tyson?*" I ask, praying that I heard her wrong.

She nods, a placid, patient smile on her face. "Yes. He's going in Erin's place and will make the pitch she put together. And *you* are going to pose as his girlfriend."

5

Too Good to Be True
Dina

I choke on the tea I just sipped and cough.

She hands me a napkin, and I dab my lips and catch my breath. I should have known it was all too good to be true. If she'd told me I was going to be drawn and quartered, my reaction would have been less extreme. "His girlfriend?"

"Only for the sake of appearances. I've had my team create your backstory, and a file on the attendees we're aware of has been emailed to you."

"Why do I have to be his girlfriend and not just his colleague like Derrick was going to be?"

"Derrick wasn't going to be her colleague. Partners and spouses were invited, and he was going as her date. Little did I know they wouldn't be pretending. And trust me, you'll get more out of them if they think you're a hot piece of ass instead of a professional."

I'm used to her blunt, sometimes callous way of communicating, but her lack of outrage at what she just described is too much. "Why would we want to do business with people like that?"

"Because we're a business. Until we can wish the leaders we want into existence, we'll have to work with what we have. I thought about sending Tyson alone. I think he could handle it all, but he's friendly with Dupont's son, and I don't think he'll be capable of the objectivity needed for proper due diligence."

I nod. I understand why she wants me to do the digging, but there's got to be a way to do it without actually spending time with Tyson. "Wouldn't it be easier if I worked more like an advance team? Dig around and make sure he has everything he needs for the meeting on—"

"If you're his girlfriend you'll have access to spaces that we'd otherwise have to hire someone to enter in less than ethical ways. Like their offices at the manor."

Her expression loses all its softness, and she holds a finger up when I open my mouth to protest again. "This isn't a strategy session. My team and I have already decided that this is the best way forward. If I want your input, I'll ask for it."

Chastised, I clear my throat and nod. "I understand."

"I know you do. I also know that you and Tyson don't get along. Which is bizarre because you're both such smart people."

"I don't have a problem with Tyson," I rebut quickly, my heart racing.

One arched brow wings up, and she narrows an eye at me. "I wasn't asking, Dina. I have eyes and a brain. And I don't expect everyone to like my children—hell, I don't like them all the time."

My heart is in my throat, but I nod slowly. I didn't know she had a clue about the tension between us. I would die if she also knew why.

"I understand why you just did it, but don't lie to me again, Dina. If you do, and I find out—and I always do—I won't trust you anymore. And I can't work with people I don't trust. Do you understand?"

I take a deep breath. "I do."

"Good. Because Derrick's role oversees the entire company, Paris included. As managing director of that office, you and Tyson will work together on a regular basis. Take it from someone who has to juggle my personal feelings with what's best for the company every day, I understand it's not easy. But if you want to succeed in business, you'll need to learn how to do it."

"I won't let my personal feelings get in the way of this job. I'll bring the same professionalism and preparation to this assignment as I do everything else."

"I expect nothing less. Now I'm going to call Tyson, get him up to speed."

Discomfort makes me shift in my seat. I close my portfolio. "I'll leave so you can talk to him privately."

"No, stay. We'll need to talk through a few things together. Give me a few minutes to send this email and we'll call." She turns to her computer. I can't scream out loud, but I let my mind have it.

I wasn't just blowing smoke when I told her I wouldn't do anything to jeopardize my job here. Without it, I'd still be stalled out in a puddle of my failures and regrets.

I'd rather stick pins under my fingernails than talk to Tyson. But I've learned that the true test of how important something is to you isn't how hard you're willing to work for it, it's how much you're willing to suffer.

So I'm going to sit here, take notes, and ask questions.

Tomorrow, I'll go to Paris and make everyone think I'm his girlfriend and make sure the company we're thinking about buying is sound.

But it's going to be hard as hell. Surrounded as I am by his family, it's impossible to pretend he doesn't exist, and there's always something to remind me of him. So despite the months that passed since I saw him, the burn of humiliation of the things I said and the rejection he dealt me still sit a little too close to the surface.

"Siri, call My Baby."

Surprised that she's calling Max while I'm sitting here, my head whips up. But before that surprise can settle, the call rings once and goes to voicemail.

"You've reached Tyson, I'm not available to take your call. If you'd like me to return it, send me a text. Otherwise, leave me a message at the beep."

"I've told him to change that absurd message a hundred times," she grumbles and disconnects.

I press my lips together and drop my eyes to my notebook, scribbling gibberish until I'm sure I've got control of the laugh that wants to burst out of me.

Tyson is My Baby. Not Max. I already know he's not the unflappable, untouchable, ruthless task master he wants the world to believe he is. But hearing his mother call him My Baby almost makes me sad that he didn't answer.

Almost. Mostly, I'm just relieved. "I guess we'll have to do this by email, then." I drop my notebook into my tote bag.

"No, just a minute. His phone is always on that ridiculous do not disturb. He'll see it and call me back. You can work in here until he does."

Like hell. I shoot out of my seat and start backing toward the door.

"I need to be connected to the VPN to access some of my databases, and the list of attendees is long."

She glances irritably at her computer screen.

My heart is racing. He could call back any second, and I don't want to be here when he does. "I'll just go get started. If he calls, you can ask Emily to patch me in."

"Fine. If I haven't heard back by noon, I'll start an email thread."

"Thank you, I'll look forward to it." And then pray like hell that whatever he's doing keeps him until then.

6

I Guess That Backfired
Tyson

I checked my phone after a long morning of meetings to find a text from my mother that said,

I don't know why you never answer your phone. Check your email, I have an assignment for you.

I only read the first paragraph before I stop and call her back.

She answers on the first ring, and then my phone starts to alert me that she wants to FaceTime.

"I read your email, and I'm confused," I say as soon as I see her face.

Her dark eyes narrow, and she purses her lips. "There was nothing ambiguous in that email. What exactly is confusing you?"

I square my jaw and shake my head. "Why am I going to do Erin Canterbury's job for her? Didn't you hire her over me because you thought she was a better candidate?"

"She's been terminated."

I almost drop my phone. "What? When?"

"Officially, today."

"Why?"

"She violated the terms of her contract. That's all I can say for now. Do you have any more questions?"

"Yes, why do I need a date?"

"She's not really your date. She's only pretending to be so that you can focus on what you do best."

"Okay, but why *her?* I have a dozen women I can call right now who won't require you to buy a train ticket and pay through the nose for a hotel." The last thing I need is Hurricane Dina's fine ass anywhere near me and my neatly ordered life.

"Besides the fact that espionage is her trade, I think she's exactly who people would expect Tyson Wilde to be with if his taste in women reflected his taste in everything else. And unlike any of the women *you're* likely to have on speed dial, I know we can trust her."

I grit my teeth. "That was ten years ago. When are you going to stop throwing that back in my face?"

"Well, Tyson, people don't change. You lose focus when your feelings are involved. So think of me sending Dina as me giving you the support you need to be successful."

"Right." If only she knew that success is the very last thing Dina is wishing for me right now.

I cross my arms over my chest and lean back in my chair. "Good luck convincing *her* to do it."

She mimics my pose. "You can wipe that smirk off your face, I already have." Her smile is gloating.

I sit up straight in my chair, beyond the point of feigning nonchalance. I thought hell would freeze over before Dina would agree to come within ten feet of me. "Did she ask for a raise first?"

"She smiled and thanked me for the opportunity. Unlike you, she understands the meaning of the word employee."

I stiffen at the underlying implication in her tone, but I don't take the bait. I don't have time for the argument that would lead to. "I didn't say no. I just voiced my objection. I don't think I need her, but if you do, then fine."

"That's good to hear." Her imperious nod of approval is the same one she used to give me for eating all my vegetables. She has never stopped seeing me as the child who needed a lot of help.

I'm ready for the call to be over. "Fine. So besides going to butter him up so he'll want to sell the business to us, we want to make sure we get information that he might not have disclosed?"

"Precisely. Dina will arrive tonight—"

My stomach dips. This is happening too fast. "Tonight? I thought you said Friday night."

"That's when you need to be at Le Meurice—that's where you're staying. But she'll need the day to shop for her weekend wardrobe."

I snort a derisive laugh. "Oh, so that's what it's costing you. A weekend at Le Meurice, shopping in St. Germain with your black card, a night at a chateau. Is she coming over on the company jet, too?"

"No, she'll take the Eurostar just like everyone else. Now I want you to listen carefully to what I'm about to say, *son.*" Annoyance tightens the light lilt of her watered-down Jamaican accent. "Whatever your personal feelings for Dina are, put them aside. You will need to work *together* to make this happen. You will also need to convince your friend that you are a couple. If his father gets wind that we're spying on him, poking around in places he hasn't invited us, it won't matter how competitive our bid is. He won't want do business with us."

I laugh and shake my head. "We won't drop our cover, but George wouldn't say anything if he caught wind. He wants this to happen."

"Did he tell you that?"

"Yes. Dupont Senior is holding this meat market to make himself feel like he's a hot commodity. And wasting a fuck ton of money doing it in France instead of in the UK. But who else could give them the placement, the reach, the white glove service we can? No one. We're the assets in this relationship. *They* need us."

She shakes her head in disappointment. "You still have so much to learn. Dupont isn't low hanging fruit. They're a wildly successful brand that has created a cult-like following. And we need this acquisition to hit our expansion targets. We may be the top dog now, but we won't stay there by resting on our laurels."

I stifle my groan of frustration at that self-inflicted dressing-down.

"Now that you know what's at stake for the company, do you want this assignment, or should I find someone else?"

"Of course, I do."

"Good. Now, when all the details are settled, I'll have Emily send them to you."

My screen goes dark. I hate the way she ends phone calls. But it's not her I'm annoyed with right now. I could kick my own ass for giving her the chance to school me on what I know already.

Of *course*, Dupont is important.

Of course, we can't take their business for granted.

But the bombshells she dropped during that call knocked me off balance.

First, there's Dina. That last time we saw each other, I lashed out. She did, too. But at least she wasn't being dishonest.

I've picked up my phone countless times to apologize. But I knew what I had to say needed to be said in person. I owed her at least that much. So I stopped picking up my phone, but I couldn't stop missing her.

Before that Christmas Eve kiss, we'd become friends in the year after she joined the company. We had conversations that made me laugh, that made me think about my life differently. She's funny and smart as hell and just as competitive as I am.

I want the chance to apologize face-to-face. I thought that would happen next time I was in Houston. I'm not prepared right now, and I have no idea what I'll say to her or what she'll say to me.

And then there's the news about Erin Canterbury—or as Fatima calls her in a show of solidarity, Ms. *Cunterbury*—is the person my mother hired instead of me. How ironic that I'm being asked to step in and save her ass.

The intercom on my desk buzzes. "Yes, Fatima?"

"Mr. and Mrs. Rivers are in the lobby. I've ordered lunch to be brought up in fifteen minutes. But I wanted to make sure you still wanted to eat here."

I glance at my watch in surprise. The day is flying. I'm having lunch with my sister Regan and her husband, Stone. They're passing through Paris to pick up Regan's kids after they spent the month with her ex-husband. "No, book us a table at Farnesina."

"Would you also like a car?"

"No, we'll walk." I know Regan will complain every step of the way, but after that conversation I need some fresh air.

* * * *

"This is delicious," Stone says around a mouth full of pasta.

"I know. The food is the best thing about living here."

His expression turns thoughtful. "Is it, really? I would have thought it was being out from under your mother's thumb."

"Well, that backfired spectacularly. She acts like one of my job descriptions is to step and fetch for her. She pulled me off my desk this weekend."

"Oh, yeah. As if you're really upset that you get to spend the weekend playing house with Dina."

I scoff. "News travels fast. I wouldn't be surprised if you knew before I did."

"Mom texted me when we were walking over. She said she needed the glam squad at Le Meurice on Friday. I have to pull some strings to make it happen, but I'd do anything for my girl, Dina."

I curl my lip in disgust. "It's damn disloyal for you to be so cozy with someone who hates your brother."

She smiles at me over her wine glass. "She hates you as much as you hate her."

"And he doesn't hate her at all," she and Stone sing song in unison.

I shake my head and scowl at them. "It's really knives out on Tyson today, isn't it?"

"No, man. It's nothing but love." Stone winks and takes another bite of his pasta.

"Well, you're wrong. To hate her, I'd have to care about her. And I don't. Like every woman with eyes, she's obsessed with me. That's it."

Regan and Stone exchange a look. It's brief, but I catch it. "What was that?"

"Nothing," they respond in guilt-laden unison.

I put my fork down and look between them both. "Say whatever it is your symbiotically connected minds are thinking, weirdos."

They exchange another look before Regan reaches across the table to take my hand. "It's okay to have feelings for her, Ty."

I yank my hand away with a loud scoff and laugh in dismissal, ignoring the way my stomach flips at her words. "I know that. I just don't think I can have a great relationship and the kind of career that will lead me to where I want to be—running Wilde World."

Regan narrows her eyes. "Tyson, that was what you said when you were ten. Are you sure it's still what you want?"

"Yes. I mean, I guess. I don't know. I've had thoughts of leaving, starting something of my own. But I can't imagine it." *Especially not now that the COO role is open.* "Either way, I'll need all my focus."

She sighs. "Fine. I don't know why you think you have to choose one over the other."

"Show me someone who has success and love." I raise my eyebrow in challenge.

"Me, Stone, Remi, Kal, Mom, Beyonce and Jay-Z," she counts off on her fingers.

"I mean, at the same time. All of you, and B and J included, downshifted when you got married. I haven't even hit my stride yet."

"Um, you're the youngest managing director at Wilde World."

I dismiss that with a wave of my hand. "But that's not everything I want. I still need to focus. When I've achieved my goals, I'll think about love."

"By then, you'll be balding with a gut. And the only women who will love you then are the ones who want your money." She smiles sweetly and bats her lashes at me.

I roll my eyes. "You're such a little shit, Regan."

"I'm just saying," she says with an unapologetic shrug.

"Babe, you're not helping." Stone gives her a stern glare and then smiles at me. "Listen, Ty, don't think so hard about it. You and Dina are both professionals, you'll do your jobs. And whatever happens with the rest is what's meant to be."

"Thank you for being rational, Stone." I give Regan a pointed look, and she sticks her tongue out at me. Stone was my best friend before he was her husband, and moments like this are the reason. He knows when to push and when to back off. Something neither of my siblings seem to have figured out yet.

"So tell me how many new locations you guys have opened."

"Fifteen. We've been trying to source from woman and minority owned food businesses across Europe and man, we're spoiled for choice. We're meeting the market where it is with what we're stocking in these stores."

"I swear you could sell water to the sea. That's incredible, and your passion for it is obvious. I'm glad to see you landed on your feet here," Stone says. Even though I know he's laying it on thick, it's nice to hear someone say I'm doing a good job.

I know signing Dupont will get press, but it's window dressing as far as I'm concerned. The real value and the thing that makes us unique in this marketplace is what people find on our shelves—things from the homes they left behind, things they've always wanted to try. Affordable, but feels like luxury because we make it feel like that.

As I walk back to my office, back up the Champs-Élysées where I both live and work, I pay closer attention to the energy around me. This city has a vibe—romantic, modern, alive. But it's missing something.

After the job I pinned my hopes on fell through, I came here to rebuild my momentum and to get some space.

I was in the prime of my life, unapologetically ambitious, and wasting time. But the most drastic aspect of this move was that I moved at all. I'm good at it but could also do it with my eyes closed. I've been bored since the month I got here.

As soon as Erin's job is posted, I'm going to apply. I know there will be a lot of strong candidates for it. Wilde is a great place for a sales professional to grow. But this time, it's mine.

I won't even waste time checking and measuring where I line up against everyone else. I don't need to. My superpower is stamina—I can outlast the strongest, outthink the smartest, and outrun the fastest. When I put in the work, no one can touch me. And this weekend, I intend on exceeding expectations.

Feeling like I earned it, I duck into Lenôtre and buy a slice of their chocolate cake. It's made with chocolate mousse and meringue and is the most delicious chocolate I've ever tasted.

Paris certainly has its charms. I'm glad I've had the experience—it's given me a lot of inspiration for the future of our business—but I feel more like a visitor than I do a resident.

As much as I thought I needed to get away, I miss Houston. And Rivers Wilde is home.

So I'm going to shoot my shot, and not even temptress extraordinaire Dina Lu is going to distract me.

7

La Douleur Exquise
Dina

My phone's incessant ring pulls me out of a deep sleep. I lift one heavy lid slowly and groan when I encounter the same dark room I fell asleep in. That means I haven't been asleep long enough at all. I caught a later train than I planned and got into Paris close to ten p.m. I hadn't been able to keep my eyes open on the train, and work I'd neglected was waiting for me. I checked in, skipped dinner, and got to work.

I resent all the paperwork my current role comes with. I spend more time as a pencil pusher than an investigator these days. Instead of getting ready for my assignment tomorrow, I spent hours approving expense reports, signing off on cases, and finishing up performance reviews that are already overdue. It was nearly two o'clock when I was finished, and I hadn't even touched the work that brought me to Paris in the first place. I worked until my eyes refused to stay open. It was almost three a.m. the last time I glanced at the clock.

I grab my phone and answer without bothering to check the caller ID. Without my glasses or contacts, I wouldn't be able to tell anyway.

"Did I wake you?" Regan's cheerful soft voice is another kind of wake-up call.

"What time is it?" I ask and peer out into the dark room.

"It's almost six a.m. I'm sorry to call so early, but we're up and about to head to the airport. I didn't know if I'd have another chance to talk before we take off, and I wanted to give you the details for the stylist I hired for you today."

"Why are you whispering?"

"We're in the car and the kids are asleep. Can you talk?"

I sigh and resign myself to having this conversation. "Thanks so much for setting that up, but it's not a big deal. I can do my hair myself."

"I'm sure you can. But this will save you time, and she's really good. She'll roll you and blow you out in an hour flat. Besides Tanaka, she's the only person who I let touch my hair."

"Well, that's saying a lot." Tanaka is the stylist she brought home from Paris when she moved back after living here for five years, and she's incredible. Anyone Regan compares to her has to be great. And we have similar textured hair. But I have a phobia about people coming close to my head with hot things. "Fine, but tell her no hot combs."

"Ear tips or scalp?" She chuckles, but I hear the empathy in her voice and am so glad I don't need to say more.

"Both," I moan.

She groans. "Same. Just talking about it is triggering, right? Don't worry. You're in good hands with Chantelle. What time are you meeting Marisol?"

"Who's Marisol?"

"The personal shopper my mother is sending you to."

"At ten a.m. Even though it all feels like a lot." Heat floods my face when I remember Tyson's quip about my wardrobe.

"It'll save time, too. She'll have stuff pulled and ready to try on. And you can just pick what you want, and they'll deliver it a few hours later. Or sooner if you need."

"Like Rent the Runway?"

"With a personal touch. She's great, and has a flair for finding sexy, flattering, tasteful things."

"I hope she knows she's not dressing one of you and that no bra isn't an option." Regan and her mother are both long and lean. I'm short and outrageously curvy. I've yet to find a blouse I didn't need to pin closed to keep it from gaping over my breasts.

"Oh, please. You've got such a sexy body. And I would kill for those gravity defying tits and ass of yours."

I laugh. "I wish we could trade. I'd love a bra that doesn't scream over the shoulder boulder holder. All your stuff is so pretty."

"You're in the perfect place. Marisol can do a proper bra fitting and make sure you get some good lingerie."

"What for?"

"Because it'll make your clothes fall better and make you feel good, too. She's really efficient. You should be done by one p.m."

"Three hours?" I gawk.

"It'll go by fast, promise. I'll tell Chantelle to arrive by four o'clock. That'll give you a chance to eat and unwind and still leave plenty of time for you to get ready for dinner. Oh my God, Tyson's going to faint when he sees you."

"This is work, remember? We're not really a couple going away together for the weekend. I'm not going to come back to my hotel room and nap. I'll need to come back and make up for the time I lost while I was shopping. Because the dinner I may or may not be attending tonight may be a meet and greet for everyone else, but it certainly isn't for me. Tyson is there to schmooze, I'll be working. And you can forget the note to Marisol. I'm not going to use my corporate card to buy sexy lingerie. It's bad enough we're sharing a room all weekend."

"You are such a contrarian. It's your birthday, the lingerie is my gift. And don't pretend you don't want to make Tyson sweat a little," she adds, in anticipation of what she knows I was about to say.

I groan and close my eyes. "Regan, I'm terrified of being alone with him," I admit. It's the most honest thing I've ever said to her about Tyson. I haven't confided in her because she's his sister and I don't want to ask her to keep things from him. But I don't want him to ever know how I really feel. It's humiliating enough.

"Dina, I know he's a jerk and talks a lot of shit. But he's a Cadbury egg, hard on the outside, gooey as hell on the inside. And also, he knows if he upsets you, he'll have to deal with me."

"Yeah, right." I laugh at the image of Regan taking on Tyson. He's the youngest of them, but he's the biggest, most strong willed and stubborn of the three siblings.

Regan sighs. "If it makes you feel any better, he's nervous about it, too. He thinks you hate him."

"I *do* hate him," I respond sullenly.

"Oh please. Only thing you hate is that he isn't naked in your bed."

I sputter a laugh. "Regan, he's your little brother."

"He's a man, you're a woman. You guys should just have sex and get it out of your system."

I sit up in bed, laughing at how she says it like she's telling me I need to put air in my tires. "If you read romance novels, you'd know that never works."

"Of course, it works."

I scoff. "Have *you* tried it?"

"Well…no. But romance novels are fiction. This is real life."

I shake my head. "Those stories may be fiction, but in my favorites ones, the *people* feel real. So real sometimes you can see pieces of yourself in them. And I've seen myself, as I am right now, plenty of times. Heroines are infatuated with trouble on legs. They convince themselves it's just because they're curious. That if they just have sex, they'll magically be able to move on. It *never* works. They end up on the slippery 'just one last time' slope. Next thing you know, they're in love."

"And what's wrong with that?" Regan asks.

My heart does something weird, and I press a hand to my chest. "It would be like Red Riding Hood falling for the big bad wolf."

"Oh, D…I know you've been hurt. But given what you do for a living, I refuse to believe that you don't know the difference between a wolf and a lamb in wolf's clothing."

"Who's a lamb?" I nearly choke on my gasp. "Maybe you're blinded by sisterly love, but Tyson Wilde is no *lamb*."

"Yes, I'm very aware of how tone deaf and selfish he can be sometimes. And I know you're pissed at him. I have theories about what happened—"

"I'm not going to tell you if he hasn't. So please don't ask," I interject.

"It's none of my business. But… now that you've confirmed that *something* happened…it's obvious you're still unresolved about it. And he's probably clueless that you're upset."

My heart kicks at my ribs.

"I wish he was clueless." He knows too much.

She sighs. "That boy, he's so proud. But—"

"Don't ask me to forgive him, please."

"I would never do that. Forgiveness is something you do when and *if* your heart is ready. Trust is non-negotiable. Even if you're wildly in love."

"I'm not in love," I reject that with conviction.

"Okay, okay, I was just speaking in generalities. But you saw something in him that made you think you could be. Otherwise, you wouldn't be so upset with him or yourself."

Tears prick my eyes. "I did see something, yes. Once. But Regan, I've never seen it again. Sometimes I think I imagined it. We want different things. I've been down the unrequited feelings road before." I sigh.

"Ah, *la douleur exquise*." She sighs the colloquial French phrase for unrequited love. Literally translated, it means exquisite pain.

I laugh humorlessly. "There's nothing exquisite about it. And Regan, are you sure this isn't awkward? He's your brother. Don't you guys talk about this stuff?" And *he already knows too much*.

"First of all, you're my friend. I'm here for you. We do talk about this stuff, but I keep his confidences and yours. I won't tell him anything you don't want me to. But…"

"Always a but with this one," I grumble, and she laughs. Despite the ball of dread in my stomach, I laugh with her. I'm grateful to have her to talk to.

"Like you said, I'm not a random friend giving you advice. I grew up with him, and I know him down to his soul. He holds most people at arm's length for so many reasons. And it's not like he had good models for what loving relationships looked like in his formative years."

"I'm sure he has good reasons, but it doesn't matter anymore. I've moved on from it."

She's quiet for a beat. "Fine, but you didn't imagine it, Dina. He's a hard nut to crack, but when you do, it is so worth it. I *know* it's none of my business, but I love you both, and I want you two together so bad, I can taste it." She nearly groans the last part.

"Regan, don't say that," I push back hard and sharp. I have to, for her sake and mine. "I've moved on. I'm here to do a job, and that's it."

"Fine. Don't have sex with him. But if you're sharing a room with him, there's something you should know. And I know he'll never tell you himself."

* * * *

I stumble into my suite and collapse on the couch in the living room. I will never understand people who enjoy shopping. Even when someone else does most of the heavy lifting, it's exhausting and time consuming. But I have to admit, it was fun. I balked at Regan's suggestion that I show Tyson what he was missing…until I tried on the things the shopper had pulled and saw how good everything looked and how good they made *me* look. I decided that these clothes might be just what I need.

I'm not trying to tempt him, but I know he will be. And he won't be the only one. It wouldn't hurt for him to see that I'm not sitting around waiting for him.

So I went with the pieces that made Marisol wax poetic even as they made me blush. I indulged in the sexy underwear, and I did it all with an hour to spare.

I take my time washing my hair in the borderline ostentatious black and white marble shower. Clean and with nothing to do for the first time in days, I decide to take advantage of the beautiful terrace that runs along the length of the entire suite while I wait for the stylist. I slip on a lacy white romper and stroll into the suite's living room toward the French doors that lead to the terrace.

It's a huge upgrade from the hotel I booked when I was paying for this trip myself. I glance around the sumptuously appointed suite in awe. I don't want to imagine how much it's costing Mrs. Wilde to put me up here.

I stop dead in my tracks when I see a small black suitcase next to the couch and a garment bag hanging on a small hook in the bedroom on the other side of the suite. It wasn't there when I left this morning. I walk over to inspect and wish I hadn't. "Tyson Wilde" is handwritten on the baggage tags that are stuck to it.

Oh my God, I have to share this suite with Tyson Wilde.

There are two beds, and I thought it would be fine.

But just seeing his suitcase makes my pulse race with anticipation and dread.

I replay Regan's revelation this morning—that Tyson can't sleep without at least one light on—and wish I hadn't asked her to tell me after all. It's impossible to know that intimate detail and pretend he's heartless rather than afraid of being vulnerable. The ice around the part of my heart where I kept things and people who hurt me thawed just enough for me to remember how good it felt to be in his good graces.

I've got to let that go and remember that he's not for me. I just need to convince my body and my heart of that. I continue out to the terrace. The view from here is of the Jardin des Tuileries, the famous gardens my mother kept a postcard of stuck to our fridge.

The heart-stopping view was one of the things I most looked forward to seeing. But I might as well be staring at a sea of nothing for all I'm able to appreciate it now. I glance around the enormous suite and decide that whatever it's costing her, I'm going to earn it all and then some this weekend.

8

She Drives Me Crazy
Tyson

I've been dreading this moment all day. I even had my things delivered to the hotel instead of taking them over myself like I'd planned to avoid it.

But since I got in the car to head over here, I've been impatient and… excited for it.

I've been sitting in front of her hotel for five minutes. I called when we were a few minutes away to give her time to get downstairs. She said she was on her way, and we should have been on the road three minutes ago.

I glance at my watch again and curse under my breath. She knows I'm a stickler for time. She's probably doing it on purpose.

I reach inside my blazer, fishing out my phone from the inside pocket, and call her again.

"Hey," she answers a little breathlessly after the third ring.

"What's the hold-up?"

"I'm on my way. I forgot my phone in my room and had to go back for it."

There's none of the telltale background noise you'd expect in a hotel lobby. "Are you at least downstairs yet?"

"Yes, Tyson. I'm downstairs. Jeez," she snaps and then hangs up.

She's going to make me crazy. I'm just about to call her again when the car door opens. "It's about time, woman. We can't be late to the first event of the weekend."

"Don't call me *woman*," she says as she climbs into the back.

If I didn't recognize her voice, I would have thought she was someone else climbing into the wrong car. "And what's the rush? I thought we had plenty of time."

Her question barely registers. Not that I wouldn't have been able to answer because I think I swallowed my damn tongue. My mom made it sound like she was just getting a few outfits and her hair done.

She's completely transformed herself. Her hair is pin straight and shimmers like black silk in the dimly lit dark interior of the car. The long fall of it creates a stark contrast to and heightens the bronze skin on her bare shoulders, arms, and chest.

Her outrageous curves are bound in a skin-tight leopard print dress that has little flaps at the hips and hugs her thighs like it was painted on.

I catch a glimpse of the black stiletto heel shoes with a toe so pointy she could use it as a weapon she's wearing. I don't have to try hard to imagine the things they do to her already long, muscular legs when she's walking.

The loud blare of a car horn draws my eyes up to the still open door. The driver is so engrossed by her legs that he's just standing there staring while she arranges her skirt and settles into her seat.

I clear my throat loudly. His eyes meet mine for a brief second, and I'm gratified by the flash of fear in them before he closes the door and scurries around the front to his seat.

When I was 15 I would use my fists to set a boy straight for treating a woman I cared about like a piece of meat. Now glowers and quiet but stern words in the men's room are the tools of my trade. I curse my sister silently as I prepare myself for a night of using them.

"I see you went shopping at the same places Regan does," I remark as I force my eyes out of my window.

"Why do you say that like it's a bad thing?"

"Because you're half naked, like *she* usually is."

"Thank God you're not really my date, or else I might be upset that you managed to insult me less than two minutes into our conversation."

"I didn't insult you."

She scoffs. "Well, that didn't sound anything like 'You look nice.'"

I glance in the general direction of her body and then look back at the road with a shrug. "Your dress is too damn tight. You're supposed to be convincing people you're my woman. Not trying to catch the eye of every man you walk by."

"Don't tell me how to do my job, Tyson." She spits my name like it's a bad taste in her mouth. "And for your information, I don't need to *try* to catch anyone's eyes. If anything, it's the exact opposite. I dress to disappear."

Oh, I know that. Even though it's been a long time, I know exactly what she's hiding in that oversized, monochrome wardrobe of hers. "Well, hate to break it to you, but if that was your goal, you failed."

"I didn't pick these clothes. The people you trusted to dress me did. And clearly *they* think your friends would expect you to be with someone who dresses like this."

"That's not true. You could have worn something you wanted," I protest.

"As if The Hunter's wardrobe isn't appropriate for a night out in Paris."

"I've never called you that."

"Well, then you must be the only person who doesn't."

"I'm sorry people are so childish."

She toys with the tiny gold rings she wears on both her hands. "It doesn't matter. These clothes, hair, and makeup, and the ones I wear to work, they are a uniform. That's it. I like the name The Hunter. Besides, I don't take anything you say personally anymore."

That's a slap in the face that I deserve, but damn if it doesn't hurt.

"We have a job to do, so let's just focus on that. Did you get to read the brief?"

"Yes. And you're Donna Li. School teacher from Austin. We've been dating for six months."

"Yes. And you know our hosts pretty well, right? What would they expect our dynamic to be?"

I cock my head in confusion. "What do you mean, our *dynamic*?" I put the last word in air quotes.

"I mean, do you hold hands? Are you into PDA? What would they expect?"

I shrug and resist the urge to tug at my collar. "I've never brought a woman with me to anything."

She's silent for a beat. "Not *ever*?"

"No. Not ever. I don't date. This is the first time they've met anyone."

"Oh" is all she says.

"Is that a problem?"

"No. Then maybe tell me what you think they'd expect given what they know of you."

"I don't know, Dina. I guess we can do what couples do. My brother plays with his girl's hair, touches her hands, kisses her, looks at her in a way that leaves no doubt to anyone watching that she's his."

She nods. "Okay, we can do that. If it's comfortable for you."

"Will it be comfortable for *you*?" She told me she'd never let me touch her again last time we actually spoke.

"Yes, it'll be fine. I'm an affectionate person." Her reply is curt and sharp.

"Fine, but no flirting back when someone flirts with you. It's disrespectful. I'll have to see these people again, so what they think of me matters."

"Well, even though I'll likely never see them again, same goes."

I scoff. "I don't flirt."

"Trust me, you do. Even if you don't mean to."

"Anything else you need?" I ask.

"Yes. When I reach for your hand, don't leave me hanging. It's one of the first tells of a couple that's out of sync, and the women will notice. And they'll ask their husbands who are your friends and then tomorrow, someone will do a Google search of me because they'll wonder who I am. If I'm everything they expect, they won't feel the need to learn more, okay?"

She's a little too good at this, but I'm glad she's got her head in the game. "Sounds fine. We have our story. Donna and Tyson met at a restaurant in Rivers Wilde. You're a teacher. We've been dating for six months."

"Right. Did you say our host is George Dupont, Jr?"

"Yes. He and his wife Kate are hosting at their house."

"Doesn't he live in London?"

"Yes."

She pulls her phone out of her bag and starts scrolling through. "Yup, that's what my notes say. So whose house are we going to? Let me see the address."

I bristle at the way she's barking orders. "You don't have to check. I know these people."

"Well, I don't, and it's my job to check. What's the address?"

I read it off to her.

She types furiously and then sighs. "Nope, that's not listed on the personal records we have for them. Let's find out whose place it is. Make sure it's not something they haven't disclosed."

"Well, it would be stupid of him to invite me there if that was the case. He's my friend, Dina. This is a good thing."

"Who else will be there?"

"I didn't ask. It's dinner. Business starts tomorrow."

She groans and drops her face into her hands.

"What now?" I ask.

She uncovers her face and turns it to look at me, her eyes narrowed in annoyance. "You have no clue who's joining us. He's your friend, but are you sure he's really your ally?"

"Of course he is, Dina."

"Yeah, because he's your friend," she says in a sarcastic tone that's too much like the one my mother uses.

"I know you think you're the only one taking their job seriously, Dina. But I'm not just socializing with my college buddy. He's the head of their sales division—and the son of their CEO."

"And bang-up job *he's* done of that."

I frown at her. "Sales is hard, especially when you've got a niche product. You can do everything right and it will still fall flat."

"Or you can expand too quickly and have a terrible strategy. One that makes you hemorrhage money and need to sell your family's business."

I bristle, it sounds so damning when she says it. "Whether he's been successful or not, he'll have his father's ear. And tomorrow, we'll have an advantage over the others."

"I hope you're right. And no more surprises or it's going to be a very long weekend." She leans forward and raps the partition glass with her knuckles.

When it slides down, she leans forward. "*Excusez- moi Monsieur, pouvez-vous dire à quelle heure nous allons arriver?*" she asks him how much longer we have.

"Dans environ dix minutes, madame," he replies.

"*Merci,*" she replies cheerily and then in a much cooler tone, tells me, "I'm going to close my eyes for a few minutes. It's been a long day."

I thought I'd be translating for her this weekend. But her French is better than mine—accented like she grew up speaking the language. I'm curious and use that as a way to bridge the stifling silence.

"Have you lived here before?"

"Nope. First time here, in fact."

"So how do you speak French so well?"

"My parents are from Francophone countries. They met here in college. I was born after they moved to Texas, but French was my first language."

"Oh, yeah. Your dad is Vietnamese, right? Where's your mom from?"

"Senegal."

"Have you been there?"

She sighs and raises her hand to turn on the overhead light. Her face comes into full view, and it's ridiculous how relieved I am that it still looks exactly as I remember.

"Tyson, why are you asking me these questions?"

"Because I want to know, why else?"

"Why do you want to know anything about me? Has something changed since the last time I saw you?" She eyes me with a knowing look I wish I could wipe off her face. But the only way I could do that would be to lie to her. And I've done enough of that already.

"No. Dina, nothing has changed."

She leans back and nestles into the seat. "I'm going to close my eyes again and try to get my head in the game." With that, she turns to face her window and ends our conversation.

I stare out of my window unseeingly as the city of lights goes by us in a blur. The silence that falls between us gets heavier every passing second, and after a minute, I can't take it anymore.

"Dina—"

"Listen—"

We speak at the same time.

"Go ahead," she offers. I take the opening before I lose my nerve or let myself think too much about what I want to say.

"I'm sorry for what happened the night you came to my house. I didn't deal with you fairly or honestly. And I wish I could take it all back."

"*All* of it?"

"Yes. And I wish I would've just said, I'm not sure I can take care of you the way you need me to."

She turns the overhead light on and shifts in her seat to face me. Her expression is incredulous.

"Tyson, I don't need you to take care of me. I'm very good at taking care of myself. And you've *never* asked me what I want."

"You said you want the fairy tale—white picket fence, two kids, a dog, yard."

"That's not what *my* fairy tale looks like. *And* I don't need a partner to have those things. Not even the kids."

I concede that point, it's true enough. "Then why'd you talk about a fairy tale? Isn't that how they all end?"

"Fairy tale—just means the way the world would look if I could have whatever I wanted. If I was a Disney princess, those things would be fine. But I'm not. I'm just a woman with brown skin and wild hair and more ambition than I know what to do with, trying to succeed in a world that's not designed for my success."

Minus the wild hair and woman part, I feel the same way. "So tell me—what would your life look like if you could have anything you want? At least in terms of the role you want a partner to play."

She sighs in relief, like she's been dying to answer this question. "It looks like me coming home to someone who's not upset that work kept me. It means having someone to make dinner for, but who also makes dinner for me and doesn't resent me for being too tired to eat it. It means someone who believes in me. Someone who I believe in, too. And someone who puts my needs ahead of his wants."

"That's asking a lot."

She shrugs. "Not when you ask someone to spend their life with you, and you alone, forever until one of you dies. You owe it to them to at least *try* to give them what they want, even if it's not something you want. I don't want kids. I just…my mother dying when I was so young had a profound effect on me. I can't control when my time will come, and I just…don't want to leave my children before they're ready to face life without me. But if I met someone who was all of those things and had kids already, I would embrace it. More than anything, Tyson, I want a partner who is as committed to my happiness as their own—who is as vulnerable and honest as I am."

I process all of that and how it makes me feel. Especially the last part.

"Vulnerability is terrifying, D."

"I know, and I'm not saying you should walk around with your heart on your sleeve. But the people close to you should never have to wonder where they stand."

I nod in agreement. It's not fair the way I've shut her out. So I tell her.

"I've had this plan and it ends with my mother gladly handing over the reins of the company to me."

"Okay, but…why does that mean you have to shut everything else out?"

"Because I let a woman distract me once, and it's taken ten years of really hard work to earn my mother's trust again. And I don't want that to happen again."

"I understand. And I'm glad you shared that with me. But what has that got to with me?"

"Because, Dina, you distract me. And I'm in a really critical place right now. I can't afford to fuck up or lose steam."

"And I can?"

"I'm not saying that."

"Listen, I get it. I learned the hard way that life didn't care about my plans and that if I was going to do better than survive, I needed to be flexible and learn to let go of things and people who weren't holding on to me as tightly as I held on to them."

"Like me," I speak aloud her unspoken meaning.

"Listen, Ty. Despite what you think, I know commitment can't be bargained for. And that we want different things in the long term."

I used to think so, too. In fact, I'd been so sure of it, I let this remarkable woman go. For the first time in a long time, I let myself wonder *what if.* We have so much in common. We're both competitive, we love the same books, we love to travel, and our chemistry is undeniable.

But I'd made my choice about what my life was going to be based on all the things I knew I didn't want.

I didn't want love and all the drama and disappointment it comes with. I can't afford to lose the focus it steals. And as much as I love kids, I'd much rather be an uncle than anyone's father.

I want to climb Machu Picchu, not go to Disneyland.

I want a balcony that overlooks a river of streetlights and forest of skyscrapers, not a house with a yard and grass that needs to be cut.

But there's nothing she wants that I can't give her and still do all of those things. At least in the short term. I'm still focused on my career, and it will always come first. But it sounds like hers is just as important to her. What if…

"Dina, can we start over? Clean slate? Please?"

She's quiet for a minute—and I know she's not going to say yes.

I'm just hoping it won't be an absolute no.

"I'm not sure a clean slate is possible, or wise. I learned some important lessons from this." She speaks slowly as if she's weighing each word before she says it. "*But* we can turn the page and start a new chapter this weekend."

God, I'm the luckiest asshole in the world. "I like the sound of that."

Her posture relaxes, and she smiles. "It can be a test drive for what being ambitious professionals and lovers at the same time would be like."

That's a little too forward looking for me. "And if one or both of us decides it's not for us, we have a pretty rock-solid escape hatch in the ocean that separates us." I stick my hand out to shake hers. "Deal?"

9

Lessons Learned
Dina

Tyson hasn't let go of my hand since we shook on the proposition I made. And we make the rest of the drive in silence. I wonder if his heart is beating so loudly it's all he can think about. Or is it just me who's dying to reacquaint the rest of my body with the cool, sure glide of his palm?

If it was just my body responding, I might not be worried about how long I can keep these walls up. I'd forgotten that Tyson is the kind of man who breaks through walls that stand between him and what he wants. And clearly, at least for this weekend, that's me.

I wasn't prepared for his honesty or the apology he offered, or the dose of reality he served before he shook my hand. I need to process all of those things and make sure that even if Tyson isn't sure what he wants, that I remain clear on what I don't.

I know about the woman who used him to gain access to marketing data. I read the file. But he's not the first person to fall prey to something like that. Otherwise, jobs like mine would be obsolete. But he acts like it revealed a character flaw. And I suspect his mother's reaction to it didn't do much to disabuse him of it.

I sneak a sidelong glance his handsome profile. His lashes and lips are both so lush and full that I understand why people call him pretty.

But this man is nothing close to pretty. He's lethally attractive. And from his fresh haircut to the elegant navy blue suit and silk dress shirt he's wearing tonight, he's the picture of a wealthy, successful, confident executive who has the world at his fingertips. It's a less formal look than his work suits, but nothing close to what he looks like when he's spending time with real friends.

Looking at him in this light, it's so easy see a man who has everything. Who can handle anything.

But I know better. Even before he told me so just now. I know how badly he needs a soft place to land—and how few people he trusts to say that to.

So I held out that olive branch. Because I need that, too.

The limo pulls off the road into a side street and rolls to a stop in front of a huge townhouse.

"Wow, this is incredible," I marvel as we make our way to the double-wide dark blue lacquered front door.

"Ty!" We turn in the direction of the male voice calling Tyson's name.

"That's George," he whispers of the dark-haired man climbing out of the driver's seat of a white Aston Martin. For a family in the midst of a financial crisis, they sure don't live like it.

We walk toward the curb, where the man is leaning back into his car.

"Here we go," he whispers and links our fingers again.

"Tyson Wilde, my man," George calls as he pulls shopping bags out of the car and straightens. "Kate realized we didn't have any bubbly in stock, and I ran out, hoping I'd get back before anyone arrived. I forgot you're never fashionably late." He grins.

"Or any other kind of late," Tyson adds in a good-natured but not lighthearted way. Instantly, I understand that even though Tyson referred to George as a friend, he's not someone who'd be invited to Friday night dinner.

George makes a show of stopping short when his gaze lands on me and flashes an appreciative grin to Tyson. "And who is this ravishing beauty you've brought to delight us all?"

Tyson wraps his arm around my waist and pulls me into his side. "Donna, this walking cliché of British public school corruption is George Dupont."

George lifts my hand to his lips for a kiss.

I resist the urge to tug it away.

"The third. Not to be mistaken for the much older, much less handsome George Dupont the second, my father. And Donna, I'm enchanted."

"The pleasure is mine. Thank you for inviting us to dinner."

He grimaces. "Yes, dinner. Let's get inside before Kate starts to worry that I'm not coming back."

He jogs up the wide, slate gray steps and pushes doors open.

A petite blonde woman dressed in a black sequined mini dress that barely covers her ass is standing on the checkerboard tiled floor of a massive, ornately decorated entryway. Everything is covered in gold leaf. It's hideous.

Wow, I mouth to Tyson.

"Welcome to our little *pied a terre*," the woman sings as she trots over on heels so high her feet look like they might break with every step she takes.

"Kate, lovely to see you." Tyson bends over to kiss each of her cheeks.

She pushes herself between us and bumps him away with her hip. "Nice to see you, too, but I'm much more interested in her." She turns her Cheshire cat-like grin my direction. "I can't wait to hear how you managed to reel him in."

"She didn't have to. I fell hook, line and sinker," Tyson answers before I can think of a witty comeback.

I look up at him, ready to laugh off his exaggeration. But the smile on his face nearly brings my heart to a screeching halt at the real affection in his gaze when our eyes meet.

I'm emboldened by the ability to speak the truth I'd never otherwise utter. "It was the same for me." Heat rushes up my neck and floods my cheeks, but I can't take my eyes off his.

Kate cackles and nudges my shoulder. "Well, well, well. I'm glad I begged George to bring me along. I wouldn't have believed it if I hadn't seen it with my own eyes."

Me neither, sister.

She loops her arm through mine. "Tonight is going to be a blast. It's been too long since we've had the pleasure of Tyson's company."

There's a suggestive note in her voice that gives me pause. What does *that* mean?

"Let's keep each other company tonight. When these two get

together there's no telling where the evening will end up." *Another innuendo.* I glance at Tyson and give him a *you've got some explaining to do* look.

He widens his eyes as if he's just as confused as I am.

Kate follows my gaze and grins. "Don't worry, Tyson, I won't try to take her from you," she calls over her shoulder. "At least, not yet," she purrs in my ear as she leads me away.

10

Unexpected
Tyson

The expression on Dina's face as she left with Kate made me want to grab her hand and leave. Kate is always flirtatious and bawdy. But I didn't like the suggestive way she referred to our past interactions. We follow the women up a spiraling staircase with rails that are inlaid with what looks like ivory and down a narrow hallway toward the rear of the house. Dina's ass in that dress is distracting as hell.

"Earth to Tyson." George snaps his fingers in my ear.

I drag my eyes away and look at him. "Sorry, what'd you say?"

He raises his eyebrows and grins knowingly. "You know, I *almost* believed you when you said you'd be a bachelor forever. Should have known a man like you was just waiting for someone with the perfect ass…"

"Careful where your eyes go, man." I narrow my gaze at him.

"I was going to say assets… to come along." He laughs at my disbelieving frown. "Wow, you really like her, huh? You're only this way about your sister."

I shrug. "Yeah, well, she's…rare. No one ever made me even think about another night, much less a weekend." As I say the words, I realize that they're true. Dina makes me think all sorts of things I don't want to.

"Now I'm almost sorry I won't be at the chateau tomorrow," George says wistfully.

I stop walking and put a hand on his shoulder to stop him, too. "You're not?"

"No, the old man likes to hold court. You know how it is when your parent is your boss, too."

"Yeah, tell me about it," I commiserate, even though I don't think our circumstances are anything alike.

"I don't know why you've stayed all this time," he remarks.

I glance at him in surprise. "Where else was I going to go?" It's never crossed my mind to leave.

"Start your own thing. Making moves that matter instead of being a paper pusher."

We approach the set of French doors that Kate and Dina disappeared through a few seconds ago, and they swing open, two men dressed in French period costumes bow in greeting.

It's like entering an entirely different world from the rest of the baroque-style house. The room is huge and was most likely designed to be used as a ballroom. Tonight, it's been transformed into a dining room and lounge area. There's a live band, also dressed in blue livery, at the front of the room playing the most benign background music I've ever heard.

Half a dozen round dining tables are scattered on the right side of the room, and an array of sofas, chaises, and pillow-lined seats occupy the left half. The entire room is cast in low light with red glass sconces hanging from the ceiling glowing with what looks like candlelight.

It's hauntingly familiar, and I'm instantly on edge. I scan the room until I see Dina and Kate sitting at a table deep in conversation, both of them holding glasses of champagne.

"And that's it for business tonight. We've got much prettier things to focus on." Kate is pretty, in the same way a blue sky or a sunset is— nice to look at, but nothing you don't see regularly.

"Hey, you." Dina smiles at me from across the table.

"Hey yourself." I run a possessive gaze over her face. From her light brown complexion to her normally huge curly mane of hair, to her narrow, wide-set eyes and her lush-lipped, heart shaped but small mouth—she's a complex collection of features that tells a story of two people who crossed oceans to find each other, who hitched their hearts to the same wagon and pointed it toward an unknown future. She's a living monument to their vision and bravery. And pretty isn't a sufficient word for the marvel she is.

George and I pick seats across the table from the women, and I scan the room. Another woman dressed in a red suit stands between

George and me and lowers a silver tray that holds crystal flutes filled with sparkling champagne. I take one but have no intention of drinking it. I need to keep my head on straight tonight.

"We're celebrating," Kate declares loudly.

"Celebrating what?" Dina asks in a bubbly voice I've never heard from her before. She wears a benignly curious expression as she lifts her glass to her lips. I'm impressed. If I didn't know she was hunting, I'd believe she couldn't wait to raise a toast to good news.

"Kate, stop. You'll jinx it," George says in a voice that doesn't match the smile on his face.

"Can't jinx destiny, baby. Let's drink to it."

"To destiny," Dina cheers, and we all clink glasses. Her eyes flick to mine, and I shake my head subtly. She shouldn't ask any more questions.

She's supposed to be my girlfriend and a kindergarten teacher from East Texas. Not someone who'd be interested in business.

George takes a glass of champagne from the tray the server lowers in front of him and raises it. "To old friends and new memories."

"Ty, I miss you already." Dina pouts prettily and holds her hand out. "Come sit next to me."

"Miss you, too, baby." I ignore George's snicker as I abandon my seat and settle in next to her.

I know she's only asking me over because she wants to drill me for information. But when she gets out of her chair and slides into my lap, my arm goes around her middle and pulls her close.

"Something is up," she whispers in my ear, smiling as if she's whispering sweet nothings.

"Business starts tomorrow."

She leans away and gives me a wide-eyed look full of disagreement. But something over my shoulder catches her eye, and her expression softens into a welcoming smile.

"Another couple approaching."

"Ron, Paula, so glad you could make it. It wouldn't be a party without you," George exclaims to the people who are still behind me, and I hold my breath.

"Yes, we couldn't turn down the invitation when you told us about the fun you have planned."

Acute panic twists my gut at those names. I'd rather eat dinner with a nest of king cobras than those two. "Avoid them like the plague," I whisper to Dina.

Before she can ask why, I turn around, my expression blank while George makes introductions.

"Oh, Tyson. How perfect that you're here, too. You're always, how do you Americans say? The cherry on the ice cream," the woman, a tall willowy brunette who looks like the Victoria's Secret model that she is, exclaims in heavily accented but impeccable English.

"Indeed," Ron, a ginger-haired man in his fifties who is several inches shorter than his wife, agrees, clapping his hands together in relish. "Who needs Les Chandelles when we've got everything we need here?"

The mention of the notoriously kinky sex club, where everything is supposed to be completely confidential, brings me up short.

"What's Les Chandelles?" Dina asks.

"A nightclub," I answer flatly.

"That's like calling Ferrari a car," Ron chortles.

"It *is* a car." I stand and pull Dina up with me. With no gas in its tank and a faulty starter. "Let's go eat, I'm starved."

11

Surrender
Tyson

I'm as close to waving the white flag of defeat as I have ever been in my whole life. The entire night has been an exercise in restraint.

Fifteen years ago, I would have used my hands to deal with the nasty, disrespectful motherfuckers ogling Dina. But I'm businessman Tyson tonight. So I've spent the evening flashing menacing glowers at them and keeping Dina as close to me as possible.

Not that it's been hard. She's held my hand all night, treated my body like she had a right to it—sitting on my lap, rubbing my thigh. Every so often, without preamble, she'll lean back against my chest and press a kiss to the underside of my chin.

To anyone watching, there's no mistake that this is my woman. And I like the way that feels.

We moved to the lounge area after dinner, and for the last hour, I've had the best view in the whole house. I haven't felt this mellow and sure in a very long time. The Tyson I really am, the man in between the two everyone else wants me to be, comes together when I'm with her.

It's my MO to sit back and listen at events like this—so no one expects me to carry the conversation. I've had the pleasure of holding Dina in my lap while she makes frivolous small talk, laughs at some of the outrageous things George says, and talks shit about college basketball.

Her lush ass is planted firmly against my increasingly excited dick, and my hand rests on her torso, my fingers brushing the underside of her breasts when she laughs. I could spend hours like this. But I'm also increasingly anxious to get her alone.

The couple she's chatting with are the owners of a small chain of European specialty food shops that the husband inherited from his father. They live in Vermont and aren't much older than me. And thanks to Dina's master interviewing skills, they've told her all about how they met, their first wedding, their divorce, their second wedding, the child they lost, the house they just bought, and the vacation they've planned to celebrate their tenth wedding anniversary.

"Tyson." She calls my name and looks over her shoulder at me. "We should go to Corfu this fall. Angie says it's the best time to visit. Cool enough to eat lunch outside and not too cold at night to sleep naked with the windows open."

She gives me a suggestive smile and giggles at her own impropriety. I'm fascinated by the way her throat dances and how whatever she put on her shoulders to make them shimmer catches the light.

She's been smiling all night, but the smile she graces me with now is different from the one she's given everyone else. That light in her eyes is a sun that shines for me alone. I know it because it's the same light in me that she fuels.

"You've got the most beautiful, expressive eyes I've ever seen... They speak volumes."

My sun burns even hotter, and her smile is nothing short of radiant. "My mother used to call them glossaries."

"Yes, that's perfect."

"No, this is perfect." To my surprise and delight, she leans forward and presses her lips to mine. The feel of her lush mouth and the essence of the champagne she's been drinking is the headiest thing I've ever felt in my life. I cup her waist and tilt my head to deepen the kiss. All the blood in my body rushes to my dick, and when she rolls her hips against the hardening length, I growl into her mouth and cup her ass.

She breaks our kiss. "I'm so wet."

"Do you need to come?"

"I was thinking about running to the bathroom for that very reason."

"Dare you to let me watch," I say.

"Only if I can see your face." She slides off my lap for the first time all night and saunters away.

After spending the evening pretending to be the man who won her over and getting a taste of everything I'm missing, I'm desperate for a chance to do this for real.

I throw back the rest of my drink and follow her. When I reach the door marked *toilette* and open it, she's standing at the counter, reapplying her berry pink gloss. Our eyes meet in the mirror, and her smile is as predatory as mine.

I step into her, press my front against her back, and sweep the thick curtain of hair off her shoulder and away from her face to expose her ear. She shudders against me and licks her lips in the mirror. I press my lips to the soft, fragrant skin and kiss it. "I love the way you smell," I whisper.

Her chest rises sharply on her harsh inhale, and she turns to look at me, her smile coy, her eyes heavy-lidded and soft. "How do I smell?" she asks in a low, throaty voice.

"Decadent and delicious. Like something this big bad wolf would like to eat." I nip the silky tip of her earlobe and then lick it.

"How convenient. I'm dying to be devoured." Her siren's voice is as supple as velvet, and I'd give her anything she asked me for right now.

I drop to my knees behind her and pull her skirt to reveal the scrap of black lace clinging to her shapely hips. "Oh fuck, these are so sexy, Dina." I draw the panties down to her feet.

"I know. That's why I bought them." She's panting as she steps out of them.

"Spread your legs, baby, and rest your arms on the vanity."

She complies, and I fill my hands with her ass, pull her apart, and reveal the creamy wetness already there.

"Oh, God. I forgot how much I love this pussy," I groan before I lick her from her clit to ass, dipping my tongue inside her just for a moment on my way.

She moans and spreads her legs even wider. I eat her from behind, tasting every fold, letting my tongue act as proxy for my dick and taking her up, but not letting her go over until her thighs are trembling and the only thing coming out of her mouth is my name.

Then I turn her around and lift her so she's perched on the counter. "Fuck yourself with your fingers, let me watch."

She grabs my shoulders for purchase, pushes herself farther back on the vanity, and spreads her legs wide open. Then she slides a hand over herself and rubs her swollen clit.

"I want to watch you, too."

I pull my dick out, and it's rock hard and begging for relief. Her eyes light on it and she licks her lips. "There's pre-cum already."

"I'm so close," I groan as I wrap my hand around my throbbing dick. It only takes three strokes while watching her fingers move in and out of her creamy pussy before I start to come. I throw my head back and groan, frustrated and relieved. "Shit. I haven't come that fast since I was thirteen."

"I hope Mr. Stamina makes an appearance...I mean, we are fucking tonight, right?" she pants.

"Oh, we are absolutely fucking tonight. And when we do, Mr. Stamina will make you pay for doubting him."

"I want your mouth back, Tyson."

"Anything you want," I growl before I hoist her legs over my shoulders, move her hand away, cover her clit with my mouth, and suck the sweet bud between my lips. Her trembling thighs slip off my shoulders, and her hands clutch my head.

"Tyson, oh my God. Tyson. I'm coming," she whimpers and then she throws her head back and lets out a guttural moan that makes my dick throb. It would be so easy to stand up and slide into her, but after waiting for so long, our first time isn't going to be in a place like this.

"You ready to leave?" I pocket her panties, and she straightens her dress.

"Yes. Let's." She drops a kiss on my mouth, and I take her hand in mine as we step out of the bathroom together.

"There you are." My ardor cools, and my whole body stiffens. I turn to find Ron, George, and three of the other men walking toward us. "All the oldies are gone, and the men are going upstairs to the cigar room. Care to join us, Tyson?"

"No thanks, we're leaving."

"No one blames you," one of the men quips, and they all laugh.

I notice the way they've been ogling both of us tonight, and annoying as it is to watch them salivate over someone they think is my woman, I didn't blame them. She's spectacular. But I don't like the leer in his voice.

I'm about to tell him that when Dina squeezes my hand to stop me.

"Ty, go on. You haven't seen your friends in a while, and tomorrow will be all work, at least for you boys."

"Yes, Paula's been dying to chat with you all night," Ron chirps.

"You know what, I think I'll pass."

"Come on, Ty, we're talking business. Donna will be fine without you for a few minutes," George says.

"And it'll give me a chance to get to know the ladies before our spa day at the chateau tomorrow."

I'm here to work, and I can't miss an opportunity to get a feel for the other potential investors. But it takes every ounce of discipline I have to walk away when my gut is screaming at me to take her hand and just walk out of here and not let her spend a second alone with Paula.

If nature hadn't made me a private person, my life experience would have. Since that debacle with Kayleigh, I've been very careful. Except on the night I met these two. I'm not ashamed of my appetites, but I regret the night I met them more than almost anything else I've ever done.

George nudges my shoulder. "Come on, lover boy. She'll be here when you get back."

12

Share and Share Alike
Dina

"So is it love?" I look up in surprise at Kate's question. I didn't even realize she had come to sit next to me.

After that strange woman Paula finally took the hint and stopped talking to me, I let my mind wander.

"I'm sorry…what?"

She laughs. "The champagne is going to your head?"

I look at the empty glass in front of me and laugh with her. It's not the booze I'm drunk on. After what Tyson just did to me in that bathroom, my mind is a scattered mess. I was so turned on by how possessively he was holding me, looking at me, touching me, from his dick being hard and hot against my thigh that I was going to the bathroom to relieve the pressure building in my core so I could focus.

When he stepped into the bathroom after me, I was surprised but relieved that he'd needed to touch me as badly as I'd needed to feel him. That orgasm he gave me with his wicked tongue and clever fingers disordered my mind. I would have let him take me in that bathroom if he'd tried. And when we stepped out into the hall, I was fantasizing about riding him on the car ride home.

"So what do you do when you're not bringing Tyson Wilde to his knees?" she asks.

"I'm a teacher," I answer shortly and then get the attention of a server to ask for a glass of water.

"Oh, I see. How nice. So where did you meet?"

"His sister and I are friends."

Her eyes move to my breasts, and she smiles. "I can see why he likes you."

I cross my arms over my chest and flash a non-committal smile. "Well, he's a man."

Before tonight, I might have thought the same—but now, I know that it's my eyes that Tyson likes best. The look on his face when he'd said that tonight made my heart skip a beat.

"You must give me the name of your doctor. I've decided to give myself a full body for my fortieth, and your ass is exactly what I want."

"Sorry, love, this is all DNA and yoga."

"Come on, you can't be wearing a bra with that dress and they're so round."

I shrug. "The dress has built-in support. Otherwise, I never leave the house without a bra."

"I'll let you have your secrets now, but before we leave Fontainebleau tomorrow, I'll get it out of you."

I'm not even offended that she doesn't believe me. I'm used to it now. In the age of the Kardashians, the figure that I've been teased for since my breasts and ass ballooned at the age of twelve is suddenly *en vogue*.

People ask if I'm wearing a waist trainer. I've come to accept the lingering stares at my hairline when people try to detect the tell-tale lace of a wig because, as I've heard countless times, "All of that can't possibly be yours."

Kate doesn't ask about my hair, but when she finally looks me in the eyes and notices their deep slant and my slim upper lid, I answer the question I can tell she's dying to ask.

"My mother is from Senegal, my father from Vietnam."

Her eyes widen, and she smiles. "Oh, yes, so exotic."

I bristle at the use of that word—I find it so offensive. I may not look like everyone else, but who does? I decide to go back to tuning her out as she starts to dissect the rest of the women in the room.

I let my mind drift back to Tyson and how reluctant he'd been to leave me just now.

That wasn't an act—he looked like he wanted to take my hand and spring down the hall. From a commitment-phobic man who refuses to admit he even still wants me, it feels like a breakthrough.

Maybe all he needed was to see that he could be with me and still do his work. What it would be like to be someone's man.

"So has Tyson told you about Les Chandelles?"

Her mention of this place jogs my memory and pierces through the fog of lust in my mind. I remember how tense Tyson became when that name was mentioned earlier. I made a note to ask him. But the way Kate's eyes light up makes me afraid to know. I ask anyway. "What is this place you all seem to love so much?"

"It's Paris's premier kink club. No bullshit, no limits, just sex however and with whoever you want—well, as long as they want it too. And if you don't want it, you can watch."

"And Tyson goes there?"

"Yes. I can't believe he hasn't taken you—his dick is a legend in that place."

"Really?" You could knock me over with a feather for how shocked I am to hear that.

"Well, it used to be. He hasn't been in a while. I guess now we know why."

"And you…watched him?"

She nods. "One night, a group of us went. He'd just come back from the States. We flew out for his first weekend. And he was in a mood, going on about some woman."

I perk up. "What woman?"

"Someone he said was so obsessed with him that she showed up at his house and cried when he asked her to leave." She laughs and shakes her head. "I mean, he's delectable, but women should have some pride, no?"

"Yeah." I smile shakily and pick up my water to quench my suddenly dry throat. I feel like I've been kicked in the gut. Is that how he talked about me and that night at his house? That fucking liar.

"What else did he say?" I ask her.

"Nothing else because I got on my knees and put that beautiful cock of his in my mouth and took his mind off it all."

"You did *what?*" The water I just sipped sprays out of my mouth and all over her face. Immediately regretting my outburst, I glance around for a napkin. "I'm so sorry."

"It's fine. And it was before you," she drawls and grabs my wrist to stop me.

I pull my wrist out of her grasp and sit back. "I'm just surprised. I thought you and George were married."

She smiles and swipes a thumb over her chin and lips, and then to my continued shock and awe, slips it into her mouth and sucks it. "We are, but it's what he likes—to watch while someone fucks me. And oh my goodness, Tyson was spectacular."

My chest hurts like I've been kicked in the ribs. Tyson had *sex* with *this* woman? After he told her I was obsessed with him. I'm horrified by the tears that prick my eyes. I can't believe I thought at the very least he respected me.

"I can't wait for more tonight."

My hurt forgotten, I lean away. "More of what?" I ask, sharp.

"Oh dear, I've shocked you." She takes my hand and strokes it soothingly. I don't even have the energy to pull it out of her grasp.

"You'll see how hot it is to be watched while you're fucking."

Dread pools in my stomach. "Um, I'm sorry. What are you talking about?"

Her blues eyes widen in surprise that I can tell is feigned. "Didn't Tyson tell you what we were doing tonight? We're sharing."

* * * *

I moved through several emotions in the span of a few minutes. Disbelief, disappointment, anger, denial, and have been in the grips of a need for vengeance for the last thirty minutes.

Because Kate almost had me. I believed everything she was feeding me until she said Tyson agreed to share me. I knew she was lying. There's no way Tyson would let someone see me naked, much less touch me. So instead of sitting here fuming at him the way I think she intended, I'm determined to find out why she's making things up.

"You do this every time you meet?" I ask.

"Well, almost every time."

"I heard George mention you're not coming to the chateau tomorrow. Did you fly in from London just for this? You mentioned celebrating something."

She grins and puts her drink down. "Okay, I'm dying to tell someone, but you can't say anything. Tomorrow, George is going to…"

"Is everyone ready?" George's voice booms over the background noise of conversation, and we both look toward the door. The men are back, and Tyson is striding over, his expression thunderous as he approaches me.

"We're leaving."

Tyson grabs my hand and pulls me to my feet. I want nothing more than to get away from these people, but Kate was about to tell me something I think she wasn't supposed to. Something that I think we need to know.

I sidle closer to him, bite my lip, and look imploringly into his eyes. "But I'm curious, Ty."

"Yeah, Ty. Share your bounty," George cajoles.

His eyes narrow, and his jaw hardens. "No, actually, I *don't* want that."

"What does *she* want?" That comes from Ron as he runs bold, lascivious eyes over my body. I have no intention of letting any of these people touch me, but Tyson won't know that.

"Yeah, babe, what about what I want?"

"The only dick *you* want is attached to me."

"I mean, yeah…on a normal night." I smile at the group of onlookers and then bat my lashes up at him, ignoring his thunderous expression. "But we're in Paris for a reason, remember?" I widen my eyes and hope he understands what I mean.

"Oh, what's that?" Kate asks.

"It's my birthday this weekend," I reply, and then I look back at Tyson. "Please? I want to see what all the fuss is about."

"Me, too. I've been dreaming about what her ass would look like naked and bouncing on my cock." This comes from Ron, and I'm so shocked by his brazen words that I don't realize Tyson has let go of me until he's standing in front of Ron, with the small man's collar in his fist, dragging him to his feet.

What the hell? I rush over. "Tyson, stop."

He ignores me. "You better never even look at my woman again, Ron. I want you to purge that image of her from your mind. I don't give a shit what you do with your woman, but I don't share what's mine." He lets him go, and ignoring everyone else, turns to face me.

The anger in his eyes is so fierce, I take a step backward.

"I said we're leaving. Now."

He stalks over to me, lifts me off my feet, and throws me over his shoulder like a sack of rice.

"Tyson, what the hell?" I wiggle, trying to slide off. The arm banded around my thighs tightens to hold me in place. With his other hand, he smacks my ass hard enough that I freeze, shocked both by the sting and his audacity.

He takes advantage of my stillness and rushes down the last flight of stairs and sets me on my feet. He straightens to his full height, and his dark eyes go cold and hard like chips of coal instead of the glittering onyx they've been all night.

"We are working, Dina. When I tell you to do something, you do it and without making a spectacle of both of us."

I am so shocked at his anger and the disrespect of his actions and words that I forget myself. "I'm not the one who forgot that we're working. And I don't report to you."

"You may think you're my mother's pet because she handpicked you for this assignment. But on this trip, you do. Don't forget it's my name on that paycheck you enjoy so much..."

Then he turns and stalks toward the entrance. I glance up and want to scream when I see several heads disappear back over the railing. Great, we had an audience.

For a second I contemplate going back upstairs. But I dislike those people even more than I dislike Tyson right now. And his threat just now, however hollow, rattled me. I can't afford to mess this up, and he's right. As much as Tina Wilde may like me, he's her son.

The adrenaline that was fueling my anger fizzles. Humiliated and hurt, I do the only thing I can and follow Tyson outside.

There's an SUV idling outside the house, and a petite woman with a blonde ponytail and a black baseball cap pulled down low enough to cover her eyes is standing by the open back door. "Ms. Lu, Mr. Wilde is inside already. Once you join him, we'll be on our way." She smiles politely and gestures for me to get in, but there's nothing deferential in her tone. I can't see inside the dark cavernous interior of the car without getting any closer. Sure she knows my name, but I've heard stories of girls going missing, and I glance down the deserted street. "Tyson, are you in the car?" I yell.

"Get into the car, Dina," his clipped response comes from inside the SUV.

Equal parts relieved and annoyed, I give the woman an apologetic half smile and hoist myself inside.

Tyson is sitting at the far edge of the seat, and he doesn't say a word when I climb in. Instead, he lifts his hand and holds up his phone. I lean forward to read the message he's typed on.

She drives for my mother when she's in town. Don't say anything you don't want her to know.

There's plenty I want to say that I wouldn't say in front of his mother.

But I can't sit here for the whole car ride and not get those things off my chest.

I take my phone out and send him a text.

I am not the one who forgot we were there to work tonight. Because unlike you and trust fund baby friends that were born with gold parachutes, I earned my job.

"Hold the fuck on," he grumbles.

No, I won't hold the fuck on. You think if your last name wasn't on my paycheck - the one I earn every cent of thank you very much - that you'd be in Paris running the show?

"Of *course* I would," he hisses. The three grey dots pop up as he starts to type, fast and furious on his phone.

I keep going.

And I'll tell you another thing. Your mother asked me to come because she didn't trust you to be objective about your friends. And she was right.

His response pops onto my screen.

I'm not going to dignify any of that garbage you just spewed. If you think anyone has ever given me anything, then you're fucking blind. I'll chalk it up to the countless glasses of Champagne you had tonight. What happened in the bathroom doesn't change the fact that, while you're here, you report to ME. And if you want to have a job at all when this is over, you'd better not forget that again.

I gasp at his vitriol, insults, and threats. "Oh, don't you worry," I hiss.

I will never forget who you are again.

I drop my phone into my purse and press myself into the opposite corner of the car to put as much room between us as possible.

We ride to the hotel in complete silence, and every second that passes darkens my mood. He had no right to manhandle me, threaten my job, and lord his position over me like that.

But he wasn't wrong when he said I'd forgotten who he was, and why everything we'd done since we got to that house tonight had been wrong. He's also right that I would never talk to anyone I worked with, or for, the way I spoke to him just now.

And I have no one to blame but myself for that scene I made while we were still in earshot of those people.

The job I was sent here to do was the last thing on my mind most of the night. It felt so good to be touched, and kissed, and possessed by him, and I forgot what's at stake for me.

I can't do my job with so much unresolved between us. So I need to get this man out of my system, one way or another. And then get my head in the game.

13

Heart So Cold
Tyson

We step onto the elevator, and Dina stands as far away from me as she can. She's been seething in silence since she sent me that last text.

And I've been close to shitting my pants every time I replay that whole nightmare of an evening and the scene we made on our way out.

If there's one thing I'm not lacking, it's self-awareness. I know I take my jokes too far, forget that I'm not a mind reader, and sometimes can't see the woods for the trees. The one place I pride myself in never slipping up—at least not since the incident with Kayleigh—is with women and work.

Tonight, I've fucked up in both areas. As soon as I close the door to our suite, she rounds on me, eyes blazing, tongue ready to lash me with words that will cut deeper than any knife could.

And I don't blame her. While her anger built on the car ride over, mine simmered and then cooled quickly.

I deserve it. I acted like a caveman. If anyone put that deal in jeopardy tonight, it's me. I physically attacked a man. If he'd decided to call the police, he would have been within his rights.

"Listen, I'm sorry about the way I acted. But first I couldn't believe that you wanted to stay for that party. And then, that shit you said about my mother not trusting me. It was a low blow, but I know you were angry and didn't mean it, so I've forgiven you. I hope you can do the same and we can move on with what was going to be a really nice night."

She eyes me like I'm a thumbprint marring an otherwise spotless window. "No, Tyson, we can't just move on. First of all, yes, what I said about your mother was wrong. But I can't believe you actually thought I wanted to stay."

I throw my hands up in exasperation. "What do you mean? You said, 'I want to stay.' Why would I believe anything else?"

"The same way I knew she was lying when she said you brought me there to share me. And that she wasn't when she told me you've added cuckolding to your list of performance pieces."

Heat rushes to my cheeks at the judgment in her eyes and voice. But anger that Paula violated the privacy agreement we all signed stiffens my spine.

"I did that once, Dina. And never again."

She looks at me in horror. "He's been your friend since college. How could you?"

"What? I don't even know Ron."

"Ron? I'm talking about George." She covers her mouth as if to hold back a scream and shakes her head. "Don't tell me you fucked Paula, too. What the hell, Tyson?" She covers her face with her hands and starts to pace in front of me.

I put a hand on each of her shoulders. "Dina, I'm confused as hell. I did do that with Paula, but not with Kate. Why would you think that?"

"Because that's what she told me." She closes her eyes and lets her head fall back on a loud groan. "That *bitch*. She was lying. I knew it. And right before you came in, she was about to tell me something about George."

"Something like, what?"

She shoves my hands off her shoulders and starts to pace again "I don't know. *That* was why I wanted to stay, to hear what she was going to say. Now we're walking in there with nothing but uncertainty. I have no clue where to even start looking."

"I'm sorry I can't read your mind, Dina. You could have just said so."

"I tried, but you lost it, and now our cover is blown."

My heart skips a beat. "No, it's not. Why do you think that?"

"We had an audience on the stairs."

I wave that concern away. "George won't say anything. I'm more concerned with why Kate would sit there and spin a bunch of lies."

She stops pacing mid-step and snaps her head up, her eyes

narrowed. "You told those people that I was obsessed with you." She speaks through gritted teeth.

My stomach falls to my toes. I don't remember saying that, but anything is possible given how drunk off my face I was. "Who said that?"

"Kate. She may have been lying about the kink club stuff, but no way she could have known that I came to your house and cried when you told me you didn't want me. Unless you told her. In the car, you made it sound like you were sorry for what happened. Now I don't know what to believe."

I don't waste time trying to deny it. "It was the night after I arrived in Paris. Two days after I'd seen you. I was upset, I had too much to drink, and I don't remember much of that night. I might have said those things, but it's not the way I felt or feel."

She closes her eyes and expels a long, deep breath. When she opens them again, they're flat and expressionless. "You know what? How you feel, how I feel, it doesn't matter. We're here to do a job. Let's just focus on that."

She walks into the bathroom and shuts the door behind her. A second later the shower comes on. I follow her in. She's slipped out of her dress, and she's standing in front of the gold leaf lined sinks, gloriously naked and visibly tense.

Her bowed head comes up when I walk in, and our eyes meet in the mirror.

"Why are we fighting?"

She closes her eyes and leans back so her head rests on my shoulder. "I don't know, but I'm tired of it. I want to feel good, Tyson."

"Then let me do that."

She wraps her fingers around my wrist and lifts my hand to her breast.

"Yes, I can tell you love this as much as I do." I cup the voluptuous soft flesh and groan at the way it fills and overflows in my hand. I roll her stiff nipple with my fingers until she moans.

"Yes, Tyson. Your touch sets my body on fire," she whispers.

I expel a breath and press my face into her neck and breathe in the essence of her—sweat and sweetness mixed and heady in my nose. My lips glide against the base of her throat, and her pulse dances against them. "Because your whole body was made for me to pleasure."

She turns around in my arms and searches my face, and then cups it. She lifts onto her toes and presses a soft kiss to my mouth. But when I try to deepen the kiss, she breaks it and pulls away. She steps out of my embrace and crosses her arms over her naked chest.

"What are you doing?"

"You may set my body on fire. But Tyson, it doesn't matter when you leave my heart out in the cold."

I don't think anything has ever made me feel so ashamed of myself as what she just said.

I laugh in the face of danger, but the distance in her words, the lack of emotion in her face, is fucking terrifying. I want to throw myself at her feet and beg her forgiveness. Which is ridiculous. I need to get my head back in the game. I fucked up and let her distract me and now I may have messed up this chance.

She steps into the shower without another word or backwards glance.

I stand there unsure what to do for a full minute before I stalk out and slam the door behind me.

This is why I don't do relationships. This is the least productive day I've had since I moved here.

I can't stay in this room. And I'm sure she's hoping I'll be gone when she gets back.

I go down to the bar for a drink. When the bartender brings my whiskey, I ask him to wait a second, knock it back in one gulp, and order a double. This is a bad idea. I'm not a heavy drinker, and I know I'll pay for it later. But I need something to numb the ache in my head and chest.

I'm on my third order of whiskey when a heavy hand lands on my shoulder.

"Drowning your sorrows?" George slides into the seat next to me.

I give him a dirty look. "What the fuck was that? An orgy? Really?"

"I'm sorry, man. I thought…you know, you'd be down—"

I hold up my hand. "Please, I don't want to talk about that shit show or that motherfucker Ron. I came down to have a drink and then I'm going home. Thank you for dinner, but next time, you can lump me in with the bores and old fogies. I like my kink in private. Did you even think to confiscate phones? What would have happened if someone took a picture and it got out? We have employees and shareholders, man. We can't take risks like that."

He closes his eyes and taps his head on the edge of the bar. "Oh shit. I didn't even think about that. Man, I'm sorry. Good thing you were clearheaded enough for the both of us." He lifts his head and gives me a sheepish smile. "So did you play fuck and forgive with your lady?"

I cast him a withering side glance. "Thanks to your wife telling her a bunch of fucking lies, no. Les Chandelles was a one-time thing, and we all signed agreements. But she told her all this shit—made it sound like what happened with Paula happened with her."

His eyes grow wide as saucers. "Kate?"

"Yes, Kate. What the fuck, George?"

"No, your girl is confused."

"Uh, I don't think so. Kate and Paula look nothing alike."

"Still, she was sitting with both of them. She just met them. She's got them confused."

He sounds so certain, but I can't imagine Dina being confused about anything. "Whatever the case is, *one* of them made her think I'm some sort of stud."

He winces and pats my shoulder. "Well, we're up in my suite, so if you wanna play while she's sleeping…"

I look at him incredulous. It's like he didn't hear a word I said. "No. she's already ready to cut my dick off. But you have fun."

He smiles and looks around the bar before he leans in and touches the side of his nose. "You can drop it. I heard your fight. I know she's a decoy. You don't have to play faithful partner for my sake."

Shit. My stomach falls, and I grab his arm. "George, it's not what you think."

He pats my hand. "Hey, your secret's safe with me. I mean, even if you weren't my pal, I want Wilde to win this bid. There's no one I'd rather work with, and I know my dad feels the same."

Relieved, I shake his hand and nod yes. "Thanks, G. I appreciate it. And you won't regret it."

"We're in this together." He claps me on the back and slides off his stool. "I'm sorry again about tonight. I'll talk to Kate, see what that was about. And I'll see *you* next week when you're in London to sign the contracts." He grins at me.

I glance at my watch. "Speaking of, the bus leaves in less than six hours, and I don't want to lose my advantage by yawning during my presentation."

George snaps his fingers and shakes his head.

"Sorry, I thought I told you, they changed the time from eight to ten."

"No. You didn't tell me. And I didn't see an email either." I pull out my phone and groan when I see it's dead. Of course.

"Oh wait." He fishes his phone out of his pocket. "I have it here."

"I thought you weren't going."

"I'm still on the original list of attendees. It came through right before dinner." He hands me an email with the subject line *Schedule Change.*

Dear all,
Due to a conflict in plans, the day will begin with lunch at noon, instead of breakfast at 9. Presentations to start at 1:30pm. Thank you for your flexibility.

I hand him back the phone with a grateful smile. "Well, thank fuck I ran into you. Or else I would have dragged my ass downstairs when I could have slept in and had a leisurely breakfast."

"That's what friends are for, mate."

I wait for him to leave, down a glass of water, and hurry back up to the suite.

Dina's asleep with the light on. And I know it wasn't by accident.

I wonder how she knew…probably Regan. And even though I don't deserve the tenderness in a courtesy like this, she gave it to me anyway. I put that away to ponder later and focus on the reason I hurried back up here and the reason I'm about to wake her up.

I put a hand on her shoulder, and her eyes pop open. "What?"

"We've got a problem."

* * * *

"It was from a damn Gmail account. If that hadn't clued me in, the conflict in plans language would have. It made no sense. This thing has been planned for months. He must think I'm an idiot," I seethe at the end of recounting my exchange with George. I'm so fucking angry at him and myself.

Dina shakes her head, her lips thinning in annoyance. "I knew it. I don't know why, but clearly, he was trying to sabotage you."

"Yeah, but why?" I'm waiting for my phone to power on, but Dina has checked her email, and there was nothing informing us of a time change.

Dina picks up the pair of tortoise shell glasses on the nightstand. "I don't know, but I have a network of hackers who are going to help us find out why." She hops out of bed, grabs her laptop, and walks out into the living room.

"He is such a liar. I can't wait to see his face when we get on that bus tomorrow morning," Dina calls back to me.

I'm sure one day I'll be able to laugh at this, but right now, I feel like such an idiot. If he hadn't shown me that email, I would have believed him.

The first email that pops up on my phone screen is one from my mother. The subject line reads "Dupont - Urgent."

I see that she's copied Dina on it, too. "Did you see the email from the boss?" I ask, my finger hovering over it.

"No, but I haven't checked since before you picked me up." She taps her mouse in frustration.

I look at the time. 'It was sent two hours ago. Right as we arrived back at the hotel."

"I'm still waiting for my email to sync and download. What does it say?"

I open it and read aloud.

Tyson and Dina.
I'm emailing you the message I received from GDII. Needless to say, I am gravely disappointed. I'll expect you both in my office on Monday morning at 8'oclock, GMT. Do not be late.

"What the hell?" She runs back in the bedroom and snatches the phone from me.

"What does the message she forwarded say?"

She scrolls and starts to read.

Dear Tina,
It is with great regret that I must send you this email. We have been advised that the woman who is going by the name of Donna Li is an employee of your firm, and not romantically involved with your son. It was further implied that Ms. Li's sole purpose was to gather intelligence on the company in a covert manner. Wilde World has lost the trust necessary to proceed in any further business negotiations.
They have both been uninvited to the event tomorrow. This is

most unfortunate. But you know that without trust, there can be no business.
Regretfully.
GDII

* * * *

"That rat bastard." I slap my computer shut. "Do you really think you can hack into his Gmail? That's probably where the idiot does all his dirty work."

She nods. "My guy Tony, he's the best. And he'll get us a lot more than emails."

I open my computer again. "When your guy starts delivering the goods, let me know. Based on what we uncover, we'll need to revise our presentation, too. If we're lucky, and work all night, tomorrow we'll nail his ass to the wall."

Dina gives me a side eye. "How? We're uninvited. We can't just get on the bus and make them take us."

"I know, but I'm not some hapless tourist who needs a chartered bus to get where I'm going. You get me the information, I'll take care of the rest."

She yawns and pushes her glasses up her nose. "I'll order coffee. It'll be a long night. Tony will send stuff in, but we need to double verify everything before we rely on it."

"Okay, thank you."

"This is my job. And he's my favorite kind of liar to expose—smug, privileged, mediocre. He'll be as easy as cracking an egg." Relish lights her eyes. Her smile is as sharp as a machete.

"I almost feel sorry for George."

"He's earned everything he's going to get today."

I laugh. "Easy, killer."

"Not until he's begging us for mercy."

"Do you really think we can pull this off?"

"We're The Daredevil and The Hunter. Who can possibly defeat us?" She cackles with relish. "God, I'm vicious." She's grinning as she turns back to her work. But I can't look away. She *is* vicious. And I think I love it.

14

Fool Me Twice
Dina

"Open your email, I've sent you a little something," Tony, my Irish hacker, says when I answer his Skype call.

"You're kidding."

"I never kid when I'm charging three times my hourly rate and deliver exactly what my favorite client needs."

I laugh for the first time in what feels like days and open my email.

"My God, there are hundreds of documents." I grin like a loon as I scroll through.

My grin only widens as I start reading what he sent. Oh, I've got him. "You are a sight for sore eyes," I croon to the files on my screen.

"Wish I could say the same. You look like you haven't slept a wink," Tony quips.

I flash him the finger. "Because I haven't."

Tyson strolls back into the room. He finished the report and went to catch a few minutes of sleep and get ready. Freshly showered, shaved, and dressed in crisp dark blue slacks and a blue dress shirt that's open at the throat, he doesn't look like he spent all night working. I don't want to imagine what I must look like.

"Okay, Tony, gotta go. Thanks for the assist. I owe you."

"Well, happy to help. What you've got is plenty, but I'll send whatever else I find."

"I owe you a steak dinner next time you're in Texas."

"As if that's ever happening, it's too bloody hot. But next time you're in Belfast, I'll be happy to let you buy me dinner. I just hit send. Hope you nail this bastard's balls to the wall."

I laugh. "Thanks to you, we might just have a chance. Bye." I put the phone down and glance up at Tyson.

"He came through?" he asks.

"Yes. I was just opening the file, and we need to review and organize it. But I can give you the gist."

He sits forward, rests his hands on his knees, and nods. "Please, don't keep me in suspense."

I hand him my laptop while I give him the CliffsNotes version. "George Dupont the Third is in debt up to his eyeballs to an Irish businessman by the name of Liam McWorrell. McWorrel owns a chain of cinemas, mini golf courses, cleaning services, you name it. Anything where the wages are low and you can pay people under the table, he does it. He's also an investor. He loaned George ten million dollars for an investment in a hotel in the Maldives. The hotel is already bankrupt, and George is in more dire straits. The only real asset he has is Dupont. And he's basically promised the Irishman that he'll clear the decks of all other serious contenders so that he can purchase the business for less than it appears to be worth but for enough of a margin to pay off what George owes him."

"You're joking. He can't be that stupid."

"Oh, he is. And in here somewhere is evidence of the money he was embezzling on a monthly basis from Dupont to keep up his lavish lifestyle."

"You have proof?"

"Yes." I glance down at my watch. "It's almost 5 a.m. Do you have a ride? If you don't leave by 7, you won't beat them there."

"Oh, don't worry. I've got that covered. We'll be there before his bus even leaves the hotel."

"How…Wait, *we*? You want me to come with you?"

"Yes, of course."

"But my cover is blown. Mr. Dupont knows who I am."

Tyson shakes his head. "He just thinks he does. We're going to re-educate him on more than just his son today."

"Are you sure? I mean, we have the goods, but we still have to close the deal."

"Absolutely. Now give me what you've got, and I'm going to go through it. We're leaving here at 7:30. Maybe catch a little sleep."

I'm too tired to pretend otherwise. "Okay, I'll be meet you back here by twenty past seven."

"Sounds good."

I lift my exhausted body from the chair and walk into the bedroom.

"Dina," he calls, and I turn to look at him over my shoulder. I know what he's going to say from the look on his face. "About yesterday—"

I shake my head wearily. "We both said things we wish we could take back. I know it. You know it. I know we need to talk. But let's save our asses before we tackle anything else, okay?"

"Okay, you're right."

He glances down at his laptop and frowns. He was working all night on revising the presentation, but I have no idea how.

"Aren't you worried about how Mr. Dupont will respond when you tell him his son's been cheating him?"

Tyson's expression turns sinister at the mention of George. "No. And I'm not worried about him knowing what you do for us. I may not be the politician my mother is, but I am a damn good salesman. When we're done, he'll be thanking us. And thanks to your impeccable and lightning speed work, he'll be convinced."

"You sound so sure."

"Only because I am. Like you said, who can possibly defeat us?"

He winks and turns back to his work. I know he meant to use my words as the same rhetorical rallying cry it sounded like four hours ago when I was running on the adrenaline of my anger and vindication about my instincts. Now as the sun is starting to rise, and I've passed the baton to Tyson, my mind is slowing down and taking stock of what happened yesterday.

Yesterday was such a watershed moment. Because I realized I don't want love that I have to fight for. I want it freely given, without conditions, I'd rather have nothing than that. So as much as I would enjoy being Tyson's lover, that alone won't be enough. But I can't force him, and I'm not going to ask him again. I'm sad and tired just thinking about what a waste it is. We're good together. There's a natural ease to being with him that I don't find easily with people.

I think we could have it all. But not if I can't trust him.

I spy on people for a living, and I love my work, but I don't want to bring it home with me. I certainly don't want to have to cross-examine a man before he can admit that he has feelings for me. He needs to show me, by deed if the words aren't easy to come by, on his own. And so far, everything he's done says he wants my body and enjoys my company. But when it comes to my heart, he has no idea what to do with it.

15

The Devil Takes the Hindmost
Tyson

We land at the chateau in Fontainebleau at 8:30 a.m. thanks to Stone's older brother, Hayes, chartering a ride for us. Dina and I climb down, arm-in-arm. I'm calm and ready to handle the rush of security guards that greets us.

The first part of this wild gamble I've made pays off when we're ushered into the waiting room of a small, sunlit office at the rear of the estate.

A burly, baldheaded man escorts us into a dark, wood paneled room where Mr. Dupont is sitting behind his desk, broadsheet newspaper clutched in his large, gnarled fingers covering his entire face.

"Please have a seat," he orders. "Thomas, see that we're not disturbed."

We sit down. When he doesn't drop the paper, my patience starts to thin, and I break the silence. "Mr. Dupon—"

"Have you come to apologize for your deception?" he interrupts in a brusque, deep voice.

"No. We haven't deceived anyone."

"Ms. Li is a decoy. She's an employee of Wilde World. George told me he heard you say as much."

"She is an employee. But she's also the only real date you'll ever catch on my arm." I glance at Dina, but she keeps looking straight ahead. I'm not just saying those words. If I can help it, I'll find a way to make them true.

"So why did you say she was a teacher? Why didn't you just ask for whatever information you were looking for?"

"We weren't looking for anything in particular, Mr. Dupont. Just doing what any well-run business does, kicking the tires, looking for weak links and hidden leaks," Dina explains.

The newspaper closes with a snap, revealing a face that's surprisingly youthful. And hair that's as dark as his son's. He looks down his wannabe aristocratic nose at both of us.

"Yes, I speak," she deadpans.

His lips pucker in displeasure, and he waves his finger at her. "I'm not happy at all with you. I'd advise you to watch your tone."

"And I'd advise you to watch your son, sir."

His back goes ramrod straight. "If you've got nothing but insults to sling, you can leave." He points at the door.

"Well, then. I'll see myself out. And leave you two to finish your business. But the only reason we were less than upfront about who I am is because of the outdated notions you've turned into corporate policy."

I want to clap as she strides out, but I'll save my praise for later.

"What does she mean by that?" the old man sputters.

"She means your company has a culture that demeans women and their contributions and promotes unqualified, mediocre men. Like George, for example."

"George? He's the one who sniffed you out. If he's mediocre, what does that say about you?"

"That we're a couple who had a passionate fight in front of people we foolishly thought were friends. To be honest, we were more focused on what we discovered about him. And I have a feeling that before this deal is done, you're going to apologize to Ms. Lu. Because if I'd come by myself, we'd both be in for a very nasty surprise once your son's schemes came to light."

His face pales, and his nostrils flare. "Well, enough with the suspense. Show me what you've brought."

I hand him the report I compiled from Dina's research. It lays out everything chronologically. Using George's own words made the picture of his deception very easy to paint.

Mr. Dupont looks down at it, apprehensive more than anything else. "And why should I trust that this is true? You're saying this girl put it together. Why should I trust her expertise?"

"Because Tina Wilde personally hired her. And I am vouching for the integrity of it. That should be enough. You know our reputations."

"I thought I did. I agreed to entertain this proposal from you because your mother seemed to understand the order of things."

"She was willing to *tolerate* your order of things when she thought it was in the company's best interest. But now that I have the full scope of your business and see what your order looks like, we're less inclined to excuse attitudes that don't have any place in a modern workplace. You've got products that are popular. But with the right marketing and development budget, we'll develop ones that can compete. We don't need you. But I think once you've had a chance to read that report and our proposal, you'll realize just how much you need us."

"I need to think about it."

"Sure. Call me this evening."

"He's my son," the man says in a voice that sounds feeble.

"He's also stealing from you."

He lowers his head and nods slowly. "You'll hear from me before the end of the day."

My phone buzzes with a text from Dina.

"I'm waiting on the chopper. Sorry about that. I couldn't sit there like a good little girl for one second longer."

"I'm proud of you. Don't apologize. He was ours at that point already."

When I step out on the lawn where the helipad sits, she climbs down and runs to meet me. She launches herself at me with a cry of victory, and I catch her. We hug, and I can feel her relief as it courses through her and softens her posture. I have to force myself to let her go. "Oh my God, I can't believe we actually did it," she whispers, her fingers fluttering at her chest as she speaks.

"Yeah, me neither. Let's hope he has more sense than his son."

She hands me her phone. "I think it's safe to call him now."

We agreed that once we were sure George was too far away from the hotel to turn around, we'd call. They've been on the road for an hour by now. I dial his number, and it rings several times. I'm prepared to leave a blistering voice message, but the little idiot answers his phone.

"George Dupont," he chirps like he doesn't have a care in the world.

"It's Tyson Wilde, you lying sack of shit."

He laughs. "Oh, Tyson. Missed the bus, did you?"

"What happened to being in this together?"

"Oh please. You have always been so naïve. This is every man for himself. And you know the saying. When it's every man for himself…"

"The devil takes the hindmost." I finish the quote for him.

"Exactly. And you, my friend, today are the hindmost." He laughs.

"No, I'm the devil. And you are fucked."

"Oooh, I'm shaking in my boots." He makes his voice shake in mock fear. "By the time you catch up with us, it won't matter. The deal will be done."

"Funny, then, that I've been at the chateau for thirty minutes, and your little stagecoach is still almost an hour away."

"I've told him about you and the little spy you brought. He won't give you the time of day."

"Well, I think your father is going to be a lot less worried about my relationship status when he reads what I gave him. Especially the part about you and *Mr.* McWorrel."

"No way. The cocks she'd need to suck to get that information are on the other side of the channel. Stop bluffing. Whatever you think you know, you don't have proof."

"Well, apparently those cocks are really long 'cause she managed to get this without leaving her hotel. Let me read you a sample.

'Liam, All good. Decks cleared. No choice but to accept your price.'

"You sent that three hours ago. May want to update him now."

Dina snickers.

"It's illegal. You can't just hack my emails." He's speaking in a hushed, harsh whisper now.

"Maybe. But not more illegal than embezzlement and fraud."

"You won't win."

"Oh, grow up. I already did."

I hang up.

"I'm exhausted. Can we sleep the rest of the day?" Dina asks as we climb back into the chopper.

"That's the best idea I've heard all day."

* * * *

I dropped Dina off at the hotel and went for a run and then worked for a few hours. I took as a good sign that she asked when, and not if I'd be back, when I left her. But now that I'm walking to the hotel, I'm exhausted and concerned that I haven't heard from Dupont.

I'm prepared either way. I spent the day working up a new plan for the European expansion that gets us where we want to be without them on board to share with my mother on Monday.

My phone vibrates inside my coat pocket. I slide it out to decline the call and see it's my mother. I brace myself for whatever she's going to say and answer my phone. "I was just thinking about you."

"Well, after the call I just had with Dupont, I'm not surprised to hear that."

"What did he say? Complained that I brought a woman into his office?"

"No. He called to say he has reconsidered his position and asked for a letter of intent from us by the end of the week."

"He accepted my proposal? He's not asking for changes?"

"Why do you sound shocked? He emailed me your proposal. It's excellent."

"I wasn't sure how you'd feel about the changes I made," I admit, relieved as hell.

"It doesn't matter how I *feel*. It makes sense, and it's good for the company. You've exceeded my expectations on this one. Good job."

I feel like I've waited my whole life to hear those words but can't accept them as my due.

"Dina is the MVP of this weekend."

"I knew you two would make a good team."

"You weren't wrong."

"Tyson—" She says my name with a hesitation that's out of character.

"Yeah, what's wrong?"

"I wanted to tell you. I'm posting the COO position today. If you decide you still want it, I'll write the letter of recommendation myself."

"Really?"

"If you want it."

"I do."

"Sleep on it, you must be tired, too. We'll talk more on Monday."

"I'm on my way back to the hotel. We decided not to stay at the chateau."

"Well, I hope you do something nice today."

"I think the nicest thing we could do is sleep. We worked all night.

But tomorrow, maybe."

"Oh, that's a shame. It's her birthday today, and I feel bad that she didn't even get to enjoy it."

Guilt tugs at my chest, and I pick up my pace.

* * * *

The suite is shrouded in darkness when I step off the private elevator. The only visible light is the one that seeps under the door of the bedroom. Relieved that she's still awake and hoping that means I can start making my apologies tonight, I walk into the room. "Dina…"

My words die on my lips. The lights are on, but she's not awake. She's curled up on the right side of the bed, the cream comforter pulled up to her chin. On the left side of the bed, she's turned the corner down in invitation. I know she's naked under there and that if I get into that bed, I will spend the next few hours tasting her, fucking her mouth, her pussy, and her ass. And she would let me. Because she and I are the same kind of animal, and we don't waste opportunities when we find them.

She wants to fuck me because she knows as well as I do that when this trip is over, the lines will unblur, and this gray area will go back to being starkly black and white. Her job matters as much to her as mine does to me, and so if we're going to do the thing we both want so badly, this is our last chance.

But fuck me. I *like* this woman. More than that, I feel things I don't want to but am tired of fighting.

I'm ready to wave my white flag and tell her that. Because I would be a fool to let her go without at least trying. She's perfect for me. And we make a damn good team. But I want her to welcome me into her bed, not in spite of the way I made her feel but *because* of it.

Just like everything else I've ever worked for, I know the best things are always worth it. And I want to earn it.

So I turn out the light and make my way to the other bedroom in the suite, turn on the light, and lie down. I pull out my phone and send my assistant an email telling her what I need. It's late, but the reason I brought Fatima is because she's the kind of assistant who doesn't let things like that stop her from getting things done.

I'm going to give Dina a day she'll never forget, and when I've earned it, I'll feast until I'm full.

16

Birthday
Tyson

"Tyson? Is that you?" Dina's voice rings out as soon as I walk back into the suite. She runs concerned eyes over me. "Where'd you go?" She's dressed in a flimsy, washed to the point of transparency romper, and her hair is caught in two long pigtails. She looks good enough to eat.

I hold up the brown paper bag and the cup of coffee. "I went for breakfast."

Her expression brightens into a smile, and she walks over to take them from me. "Oh. I woke up and you were gone, and I thought…"

"That I wasn't coming back?"

She shrugs, her smile sheepish. "Well, I didn't know, work is over."

I sit down on the couch and pat the cushion next to me. "It is, but you still have a whole day. You were sleeping when I left."

She sits down, crossing her legs underneath her, and takes a sip of coffee while she inspects the bag. "This is so good. But we could have ordered room service."

"No, open the bag, just smell it and you'll know why I went to get it."

She rolls her eyes but does as I ask and then gasps. "Oh, my God. What is this?"

She pulls the muffin-shaped golden brown pastry out of the bag and presses the whole thing to her nose.

"Those are called pistachio financier, and Maison Kayser makes the best ones I've ever had. And they're gluten free."

She eyes me skeptically. "How did you know I don't eat gluten?"

"We've had dinner enough times for me to notice you don't eat bread and pasta. Take a bite."

She sinks her teeth into her bottom lip and then opens her mouth and bites half of it at once. "It's so delicious. Oh my God. Thank you. Where's yours?"

"I ate on the way back. And happy belated birthday. I hope you're well rested."

She grins. "Wow, thank you, and I am." She walks over to draw back the curtains over the terrace door, and light floods the already bright room. Behind her, the Eiffel Tower spears the blue sky and appears nestled into the tops of the bright green elm trees that line the avenue of the famous botanical garden. It's beautiful, but with Dina standing in front of it, it's reduced to a mere backdrop.

"So do you have plans today?"

I glance at my watch. "I've got to work this morning, and you've got an appointment at 9 a.m."

She smiles, bemused. "I do?"

"Yes, at the spa downstairs. It's really nice."

"Yeah, I know. I wanted to get a pedicure, but it costs more than my Brazilian wax, and they didn't have any appointments. How'd you manage that?"

"Bribery may have been involved."

She walks over, sits, and takes another sip of coffee. "Why?"

"Because I'm an ogre and worked you ragged on your birthday, and I want to make up for it."

"Wow, thank you, Ty."

"And when you're done, I thought we could have lunch at my place. It's got a great view. We can just relax and not worry about getting dressed up."

"Hunter chic allowed?"

"Whatever you want to wear is what's allowed."

"That sounds great. And what will you be doing while I'm at the spa?"

"I have to go to the office—I have paperwork to catch up on, and then I'll come back to pick you up."

"What time will that be?"

"Okay, the spa says you'll be done by one p.m., and it'll give you time to get all the works and get changed and we could be at my place by 2 p.m."

"Two? Like, in six hours from now? That's a really long massage."

"You're not just getting a massage. You're getting everything."

Her eyes bug out. "What? That's too much. Seriously, you didn't have to do all of that."

"Yes, I did. You had a long, hard day yesterday, and all I did was make it longer and harder. Time isn't on our side, but I'm going to use every second I've got to make up for that. And all you have to do is enjoy yourself. That's an order." I w ag my finger at her.

She mimics my gesture, and I'm tempted to walk over and suck that finger into my mouth. Later.

"Thank you, Tyson. This is really nice."

"So are you, Dina." That earns me a grin, and the dimple I forgot she had winks at me. "I love your smile." The words escape before my brain corrals the affection and longing they're born of. I'm grateful my skin hides my blush of embarrassment when her grin eases into a wide smile that deepens the divot in her cheek.

"I'm sorry," I continue, "I haven't given you reason to grace me with it, but I hope today is the start of me being able to make up for some of that. Thank you for having my back, in more ways than one, yesterday, D. I'm damn grateful. I hope when you get on that train tonight, my actions will have said everything I can't find the words to say."

She cups my face and searches my eyes. "Don't go to work today. Come with me to the spa. You need it, too."

Surprised, I lean away. I planned to spend some time working on proposed changes I want to make to the job my mother offered me yesterday. After my conversation with Dupont, I know I can't go back to the status quo.

At my silence, she smiles and gets up. "Don't worry about it. I knew it was a longshot, but I wouldn't be where I am if I was afraid to shoot them. I'll see you for lunch?"

She did a good job trying to hide it but I saw the disappointment in her eyes. I follow her to the bedroom and knock on the open door. "We're celebrating your birthday, so your wish is my command."

She pokes her head around the edge of the door, her smile back at full wattage. "Really?"

I tap the tip of her nose. "You get dressed, I'll call down and tell them it'll be a couple's appointment instead."

17

Concorde
Dina

I'm downstairs.

Tyson's text arrives at 1:30 p.m. on the dot, and my heart skips a beat. I've learned how anal he is about time, and even though he made it sound like a casual afternoon, I didn't want him to hurry me and ruin the absolutely blissed-out mood I'm in after the perfect day I spent at The Valmont spa. There's not an inch of skin on my body that hasn't been scrubbed, massaged, or pampered. The champagne and chocolate macarons they served while I waited for my muscles to collect themselves sufficiently to take me back to my room were the most delicious things I've eaten in a long time.

I'm not good at letting people take care of me because I'm not used to it. But I'm really good at knowing when other people need someone to take care them. And just like he said that night, even the strongest people need a soft place to land. And after the crisis we averted yesterday, we both needed it.

I didn't want to leave Paris, and him, without any happy memories. So I left the light on again and made an unambiguous offer.

When I woke up and saw his pillow as undisturbed as it was when I went to sleep, I thought he'd declined and figured it was no more than I deserved after the way I talked to him the night before.

Resigned and resolved not to waste my final day in Paris, I dragged myself out of bed and was about to order the hotel's famous Sunday

Feast brunch when he came back.

I've never been happier to see anyone as I was to see him standing there, looking so handsome in jeans and a white polo. And when he said he loved my smile, I decided in that instant that I was going to open my mouth and say what I wanted.

When he said yes, I felt like I'd won the lottery.

We went downstairs as a couple even though we didn't have an audience. Every glance, every skim of skin, every brush of our lips today has felt like a deposit for later.

An hour before the appointment was due to end, he announced that he had to leave but would be back by 1:30 so we could walk over to his place together.

I adjust the new bra I'm wearing, grab the bright yellow sundress hanging on the chair, and slip it over my head.

I step in front of the mirror to make sure it's falling properly. I've worn black for so long I've forgotten how much I love color.

My phone buzzes again, and I abandon my self-scrutiny as I hurry toward the door and unlock my phone, ready to tell Tyson to hold his horses. But his text stops me in my tracks.

Take your time. I'm easy.

I laugh to myself because I know he's not easy. But the fact that he's trying to be makes me giddy.

I slip my feet into the flat, black sandals, check my teeth for lipstick, and hurry out to meet him.

I see him as soon as I step off the elevator. He's sitting near the entrance, dressed as he was this morning. He's holding a single peony in his left hand and is on the phone. He waves me over, ends his call, and stands just as I reach him.

"Hello sunshine, this is for you." He hands me the flower and leans down to press a soft kiss to my surprised lips.

"Thank you." I take the flower and press it to my nose, breathing in the sweet smell of it before I slip it into my hair.

"You look great, smell even better. How was the end of the service?" he asks and takes my hand in his like it's the most natural thing in the world. We walk out of the lobby and step onto the stylish Rue De Rivoli.

"I feel great. It was amazing. You've created a monster, though. I'm already looking for places like this in Houston, 'cause I need a Sunday like that at least once a month."

"Regan will know." He smirks and tugs me to the right. "Come on, it's a short walk to my place, but it's packed with plenty of Parisian landmarks."

"You live that close to the hotel?"

"Just past Place de la Concorde at the Champs-Élysées."

"Oh my God, that's where Louis XVI and Marie Antoinette were beheaded."

He laughs. "You say that with such relish, and yes you're right, but then it was called Place de la Revolution. Today, it's home to parades and the finish line for the Tour de France."

"You say it like it's no big deal."

"It is a big deal, but I think the company I'm in right now is a bigger deal than all of that."

I step in front of him, plant my feet, cross my arms, and search his handsome face skeptically. "Who are you and what have you done with Tyson?"

"Very funny." He rolls his eyes, slips an arm over my shoulder, turns me around, and we continue walking. "I've never been impressed by buildings that stand exactly where the people who built them intended them to."

"What else was it supposed to do? Grow legs and move?"

"Of course not, and I'm not saying it's not a great architectural feat. But when I'm walking home from work, the thing that makes me pause, look twice, are the people that are where and what they shouldn't be."

"And…that's me?"

"Yes. But it's also me. I mean, by all rights, neither of us should be here. Not just in Paris, but even alive." He stops in front of a market with its produce on display outside. "Those mushrooms look good, right? You like mushrooms?"

"Yeah…sure," I answer absently. He calls out to the man standing behind a till inside the store's open window and orders a pound of them and then tells him we're going inside to get a few more things.

I let him lead us into the small grocery store and stop by the entrance to pick up a small basket. "Any allergies besides gluten?"

"No." But I'm still stuck on what he said outside. "Did you say we shouldn't be alive?"

He grins while he scans the shelves, pulling things off and

examining them. "I mean…My mother was born in Kingston, Jamaica, my father in Houston, Texas. Your mother was born in Dakar, Senegal and your father in Ho Chi Minh City, Vietnam—what are the odds that our parents would meet? And what are the odds that their children would be together in a city that was established by people who couldn't even fathom our existence? And yet, here we are. Together. Free, secure, and if offered an inch, we take a mile."

"Sounds about Tyson to me," I quip.

He shrugs. "Where would I be if I didn't? Certainly not in Paris, holding your hand. And you're the same way. You don't ask for permission, and you don't let other people set limits."

"You should have met me five years ago."

"Wish I had." He squeezes my shoulder, and my stomach flips. "Come on, let's go pay."

At the counter, he empties the basket, and I glance at him in surprise. "You are going to cook?"

"Why do you sound shocked?"

"I don't know…I can't imagine you behind a stove."

"Well in a few minutes, you won't have to imagine it. You eat pork?"

"Sparingly."

He glances at his watch, thanks the clerk, and scoops up the shopping bags. "Perfect, we'll make one more stop and then we'll be home."

We don't hold hands again, but we walk in companionable silence until we reach the Avenue des Champs-Élysées.

"When you come back, and we have time, we'll stop at those gardens." Tyson points to the gardens on our right.

I ignore the pang in my chest at the implication that there will be a next time—it's one of those things people say flippantly—and soak in my first time on this world-famous avenue. "Where are all the cars?"

"It's closed to vehicles on Sundays, so it's even more picturesque than usual. When Regan's kids are here, they spend their weekends with me, and I can take them there and let them play while I work and not worry that one of the boys is going to run into traffic because his brother dared him to."

"I wonder where they get that from."

"Their mother," he deadpans, but there's a fondness in his smile and in his eyes when he talks about his family that makes my heart squeeze.

Lord, help me, I'm jealous of children now. "That must be fun for them."

"For me too. And when we're all done, there's a puppet theatre and restaurants that even their picky asses like. When they're gone, I'm so tired, I usually just eat and go to bed."

I try to imagine Tyson with Regan's three kids being a doting uncle, and my heart is warmed by it. I don't want kids of my own, but I love them.

"Do you want kids?" I ask him as we walk past the giant redwoods and sugar maples that dot the border of the street.

"No." His answer is brusque. "One last stop." He ducks into a butcher shop, letting go of my hand as he does. So I don't follow him inside. Instead, I marvel at the amazing tall bronze and crystal fountains and the rose bushes and rhododendrons that create a border that breaks up the less contemporary monuments and statues.

"You ready?" He steps back out and drops a brown paper package into one of the bags from the grocery. "I'm just around the corner." And he means it quite literally. Less than ten steps away, he unlocks a black wrought-iron gate and pushes it open for me to step through.

A small courtyard with benches and trees sits in the center of a block of flats, each with a gleaming black door and large brass knocker.

We stop at a door with a 12 on it, and he places his hand on a panel above the handle. The door beeps and then glides open like someone is standing behind it, pulling it.

"Voilà, welcome to my home." He gestures for me to step inside first.

I can't hold back my gasp at the sight that greets me. It's a huge, bright south-facing apartment decorated in grays and green accented furniture and art that is a perfect complement to the high white walls and dark wood floor. It's an open concept with the kitchen, the dining room, and the sitting room all occupying the space.

"I'm going to wash my hands and get dinner started, make yourself at home. Feel free to look around. My bedroom is down that hall, and there's a small office down the other."

I can't wait to see Tyson's bedroom, but I kick off my shoes and wander around the living room, perusing his bookshelf while surreptitiously watching him in a domestic pose that I don't think I would have believed he was capable of if I wasn't seeing it with my own eyes. He whistles to himself while he puts things in the fridge and pulls pans out of his cupboards.

"Music?" He yells like he thinks I'm in the other room.

"Yes," I respond, and he spins around, surprise on his face. "I thought you were taking a tour."

Embarrassed to be caught standing there like a kid outside a candy store, I sweep my gaze over the apartment. "I'm about to. Anything off limits?"

He smiles and shakes his head. "No, I have nothing to hide. I'll get dinner going and meet you on the terrace. There's a pitcher of Bissap chilling in a bucket, glasses, and some stuff to snack on if you're peckish."

I gawk at him. "Bissap? How in the world did you mange that?"

"Fatima, my assistant, ordered the pillows and had the cleaners in so you wouldn't walk in to find it looking the way it does in between her visits," he chuckles. "I gave her the ingredient list and she worked her magic. She found both mint and flower blossom so you've got a choice."

"But…how did you even know?" The traditional Senegalese drink, made with hibiscus flowers, water, sugar, mint, or orange blossom, was my mother's favorite.

"You told me once."

"You remember?"

He winks. "I remember everything."

Clearly. Short of breath and in need of a minute away from his intoxicating presence before I throw myself at him and beg him to never let me go, I turn toward the French doors. "I'll go outside. Maybe you can show me the bedroom when you're done."

"Good call. That space is the star of this property and why I bought it. The American Embassy is behind us, and The Grand Palais is right across the street, but you can't see either of them, and no one can see you."

Curious and excited by his cryptic directive, I hurry outside, throw the doors open, and gasp at the sight that greets me.

There are beautiful, high walls, with ivy-covered trellises covering the whole space. The sun peeks through, but it's dark enough that the fairy lights woven into it are visible in the early afternoon. The seating area is a patchwork of bright blue cushions on the floor with humungous green and gold pillows strewn over them.

It's stunning. All of it. And I decide not to worry about what he's doing and how I'm feeling. I'm going to squeeze every last drop of good out of today.

I walk over to the small table in the middle and decide that today, I'm not going to limit my choices. I fill one of the tall narrow glasses halfway with the mint Bissap and the other half with the hibiscus Bissap. Then I settle onto one of the cushions and wish myself a very happy birthday.

18

Full

Tyson

"I'm stuffed. Good lord, I'm going to need to be wheeled onto the train tonight." Dina flops back onto the pillows arranged behind her and splays her arms wide.

I've been flirting with her all day. Innuendo, brief kisses, even a few nibbles at her neck, but we've only got a few hours before she needs to leave to catch her train, and I'm not wasting any more time. "There's plenty of time for us to work it off."

She doesn't respond right away, but she rolls over on her side, a lazy smile on her sweet mouth. "I like the way your mind works, Daredevil."

I reach for her and kiss her long and deep and slow. She tastes like spice and sweet and heat, and mine. I take my time, even though I know we don't have lots of it, because the thing I regretted more than anything was that I didn't kiss her more when I had the chance.

But she's impatient, and with a low growl she pushes me back and climbs on top of me, straddling my lap.

"I am going to eat you alive," she murmurs against my mouth and then she pulls her dress over her head, revealing a lace body suit that I think is the sexiest lingerie I've ever seen in my life. Or maybe it's just that on her, everything looks like that to me. "Good lord, woman," I remark and run my hands down her sides.

"I know. It's amazing what it does for my tits," she says and nibbles her way down my neck, kissing and sucking and biting my skin.

"Take your shirt off, Ty," she breathes and starts to tug at the bottom of it herself.

"Yes, ma'am." The shirt isn't all the way over my head before her lips close over one of my nipples and she sucks hard on it. "Ahhh— Dina, baby, shit."

She bites and sucks and then slides down my body, sucking and biting and licking her way down my stomach.

She kneels between my spread thighs and tugs the buttons of my pants open. "Have I told you how much I love your cock, Tyson?"

"Uhh, no, tell me."

"That would take too long. Just know that it's the dick I used to dream of but didn't think existed."

"Really?" My laugh morphs into a groan when she pulls me out of my boxers and wraps one of her small, soft hands around it. I'm already hard, and she strokes in short, fast pumps. I hiss at the sensation.

She lies down on her stomach and brings her face level with my dick. She looks up at me, and her eyes are luminous. If she wasn't still working me with her hand, I could believe the whole world existed in them. "And watching you come—oh God, the way you spurt all over your stomach, the way you're still hard when you're done, nothing makes me wetter than that. It deserves a crown."

"A crown?"

"As if you don't love it as much as I do. It's perfect and so big and long."

"Yeah, but a crown?" I laugh.

"Yeah, just like this." She replaces her hand with the hot, plush wetness of her sinful mouth and takes me in as far as she can. Then she uses her tongue to tease the underside of it while she drags her lips up to my head and then sucks on it.

"Dear God," I groan and grip the pillows beside me. She wraps her hand around the base of my cock and starts to move me in and out of her mouth, licking my head and dipping her tongue into the slit where precum is already beading.

I'm not going to make it. My heart is pounding, and the pleasure is outrageous. If this is it, I'll be ready but only after I get to the true nirvana.

"I want to be inside you."

Her mouth releases me, and she lifts herself up and straddles me. "I need you inside me. I need to come that way, so badly," she pants.

"I'm going to give you everything you need, baby." I reach between us and finger the soaked lace between her legs before I tug it to the side. She lifts and then lowers herself onto me, and we both release guttural, broken groans when I breach the tight entrance of her body.

She rocks her hips, I thrust mine up, and we come together in one perfect movement that creates an explosion of ecstasy like nothing I've ever felt. "First, I'm going to do something else I've dreamed about," she pants in my ear.

"What?"

"I'm going to kiss you while you're inside of me, and I'm not going to stop until I can't breathe. And maybe not even then."

Her lips cover mine, and her tongue slides across my mouth. I open for her. We kiss and kiss, and she rides me, setting a pace that I don't try to rush. I reach between us again and wet my finger in the folds of her pussy. I find her clit and squeeze. Her scream breaks our kiss, and her head falls on my shoulder. She moves up and down, her head falling back when I start to rub. "Yes, that's it. Yes, please please, yes. Break this wall, Tyson," she chants over and over. Then she breaks. Her pussy squeezes me in a pulsing rhythm that feels tied to the raging beat of my heart.

She trembles and collapses over me, panting and boneless.

"My turn," I whisper, press a kiss to her ear, and then roll us over so she's on her back.

She looks like a woman who's satisfied, but I don't want her to leave here feeling anything less than ruined.

I tug off the lacy bodysuit and toss it away. I feast my eyes on her for a moment before I lower my mouth to taste one of her dark brown nipples. It's unbelievably soft and hard at the same time, and I suck it deep into my mouth and play with the other one until she grabs my head and moves it.

"Please inside me, please. I want to feel you come, too."

I drive into her body with one hard thrust, and her back bows off the bed. I know she thinks she's going to walk away and leave me, but I'm going to make sure she can't help but come back.

"Tell me who has ever fucked you better than me?"

"Nobody, baby."

"Damn straight. Who could when your pussy curves to *my* dick?

When it feels so damn good."

"So good, Ty, too good."

I gather her up in my arms, lift her onto my thighs, and sit back. "Ride me until you come. And when you come, I want you to call my name like you know I'm yours."

My bad-ass baby does what I ask, and when she comes, her name is on my lips, too.

* * * *

"What do you like about me?" Dina asks around a mouthful of rice. We came inside, showered, heated up leftovers, and climbed into bed to eat.

I smile and glance at her. "Fishing for compliments?"

"No, I really want to know."

"Well, I like that you're unapologetic and not easily intimidated. I love that you ask questions about the things that I thought only I cared about. You're funny. You're ambitious. And I like that even though I don't know how to ask for it, you know when I need tenderness."

She nods and swallows her food. Her eyes are soft and searching. "I wish you'd show yourself some, too."

"I want that, too. This day with you feels like a good start."

"It's been great."

"What do you like about me?"

"I love your ambition. I love your loyalty. I love that you like to read. And I like that you try things that scare you." A mischievous smile dances on her lips. "Well, except me."

"Because you terrify me."

"Me? Why?"

"You don't need me."

She sits up. "What?"

"You said it."

"Well, not the same way a fish needs water. I won't die without you. But I certainly haven't been happy and thriving since we fell out. And no matter what, Tyson, I'll never turn my back on you. Never. We're a team, we're friends, and we can be anything we both want to be."

"I didn't know that when I left Houston."

"And what about now? Ty?" Her voice is soft, low, husky, and dripping with affection and need that makes my heart do a flip.

"I trust you. Do you trust *me*?"

She nods. "Can I?"

"Then we can figure the rest out. Let's sleep."

She nods, takes my bowl, stacks it on top of hers, and walks them to the kitchen. She comes back, lies down beside me, and curls her soft, warm, so perfect I could weep body against mine. I can't believe I pulled this off. Now if I can just find a way to make it last.

19

Buzz kill
Dina

"Oh my God, your mother's calling, Tyson, stop." I press my hands to his muscular shoulders, intending to push him off, but instead, I stroke down his broad, beautiful, sparsely haired chest. "Why did we wait so long to do this?"

He grins, and a bead of sweat drips off his forehead and onto my lips. His eyes track its movement and land on the spot of moisture. "Because we're idiots." He leans down and sucks my lower lip into his mouth and drives deeper and harder into me.

We've been making love for hours. We stop, sleep, eat, and then jump back on each other. I haven't had any clothes on since he took them off outside on his patio. It's heaven.

My phone's incessant ring starts again. "Ugh, fuck this." He pulls out of me, rolls over, and grabs the phone from the nightstand. "What could she possibly need? And she's calling FaceTime, too."

Panicked at the thought of him picking up with his sweat-drenched bare chest visible, I make a wild grab for it. "No, don't you dare answer it. Tyson, stop."

"Woah." He hops off the bed before I can grab him, stands at the foot of it, and eyes me curiously. "What? You think she won't approve?"

I glare at him and lunge up, but he lifts my phone even higher over his head.

"Approve of what?"

"Of us." He strokes his glistening, still hard dick and winks at me.

"This isn't funny. She's called three times. Clearly it can't wait." I stand on the bed and yank the phone out of his hand with a glare.

"Sorry, I mean, I figured she's going to find out at some point, might as well rip the Band-Aid off. But I understand you have a hero worship thing with her, so I'll let you set the pace."

"The pace of *what?*"

The phone starts to ring again. He flops back on the bed and crosses his arms behind his head. "I'll be waiting when you get back."

I throw my dress over my head, scrape my hair back into a ponytail, and walk out onto his balcony for privacy. And then I call her back.

"Dina, what in the world is going on? I haven't heard from you since Friday evening."

I close my eyes and bite the inside of my lip. Shit. "I'm sorry, I thought Tyson briefed you. We got back late Saturday, and yesterday was my birthday. I slept in."

She sighs. "It's fine. I did talk to Tyson, so I know that all ended well, but I expected to hear from you regarding George and the real financials at Dupont."

"I was going to give you my report on Monday."

"Today is Monday. You were supposed to be back."

"It's Monday?" I ask, shocked. How is that possible?

"Yes, it's Monday. Tyson isn't at the office either, and I thought something had happened to you two."

My stomach knots at the reproach, and I swallow thickly.

"No, we're fine. Um, sorry. I lost track of time. I've been asleep, it was a pretty hectic day yesterday."

"Where are you now?"

"At my hotel," I lie.

"Fine. I was going to tell you this today in person, but seeing as you're not here, this will have to do."

"Tell me what?"

"I'm offering Tyson Erin's role."

"Oh, wow. That's...great," I say woodenly, but my heart is beating out of my chest as her words sink in. It's not great at all.

"Well, I don't know, but he's certainly qualified, and it's what he wants. But I need you to do the background check on him."

My stomach churns. "Oh, I do those now? I thought they were manager level duty."

"This is where business and personal mix. I want it done by

someone I know won't use it to exploit him. So it must be you, please."

The please at the end is the most vulnerable I've ever heard her sound, and I can't bring myself to say no. Because I'd have to explain why, and right now, I'm not sure I can explain it to myself. "So if he takes Erin's role, that means I will report to him?"

"Yes. And thank goodness I don't have to worry about *you* two falling in love. I mean, if my son knew what was good for him and you weren't in such a rush, but alas…"

"In a rush for what?"

"To be settled."

"Is it obvious?"

"Very. But it's normal and wasn't an indictment."

"Does he… Tyson, does he know about the job?"

"Yes. I told him on Saturday that it was his for the taking."

"I mean, does he know *I'm* taking Derrick's job?"

"No, not yet. You haven't signed your contract, didn't want to get ahead of myself. But I can tell him."

"No, it's okay. I was just wondering." Because he didn't mention it. "I'm going to get myself together. I'll be in the office tomorrow. I'm sorry I fell off the face of the earth. It won't happen again."

I hang up the phone and press my hands to my racing heart. Oh God, why can't I just for once have everything I want? I'm a good person.

I sit on the floor, draw my knees up to my chest, and rest my cheek on my knees. I'm heartsick not because I'm faced with this choice but because I don't think Tyson will struggle at all when he finds out.

"Hey, you okay?" Tyson is leaning against the frame of the door I left open on the balcony. He's wearing boxers and nothing else. And I just want him so much that I wish I could roll back time and not have answered the call. "What did my mom want?"

I reach a hand up, and he takes it in his. "Sit, please?"

"Sure. Tell me what's wrong."

"Your mom made me an offer before I came here."

He frowns. "What offer?"

"Director, Derrick's old job."

He lets out a low whistle. "That's a nice level up, Dina."

"I know."

"So why are you looking like you just got fired instead?"

A laugh that has a fringe of hysteria at the beginning escapes at his choice of words.

"Because in your new role, you'd be my boss."

"And would that be so bad? I mean, yeah, I work my people hard, but—"

"No, it's not that. It's the company policy. We can't be anything more than supervisor and direct report."

"Oh, come on, they don't enforce that."

"That's why Derrick and Erin were terminated. They were together, even before she came to Wilde, and she promoted him, moved to London, and let him get away with all sorts of shit before anyone realized. They do enforce it."

He closes his eyes. "Shit."

"Yeah…shit." My stomach dips at the defeat in his voice.

"How come you didn't mention she'd offered you Erin's job?"

He shrugs. "Honestly, I haven't even thought about it since she made the offer on Saturday. Also, I just realized it's Monday morning. I thought it was still Sunday."

I groan and cover my face again. "Tyson, see that's why couples shouldn't work together. Our first attempt and we almost fucked it up and then we lost a whole day in bed."

"It is pretty damning, isn't it? Good thing I didn't answer that phone. There'd be no way to keep it from her then."

His words cool my ardor and bring me crashing back down to earth. I surge to my feet.

"I need to pee." I walk into the bathroom and sit on the toilet.

"You're not peeing," he calls from outside the door.

"I know, I'm thinking."

"About what?"

"This is my dream job, Tyson. I've worked my ass off for it. You are my dream man. I'd work my ass off for you if I thought…"

"Thought what?"

I stand up and pull the door open. He is standing there with his arms crossed over his chest and an expression I can't read on his face. "Thought what?"

I mimic his stance and square my chin. "What do you want from me?"

He doesn't miss a beat before he answers. "Anything you'll let me have. What do you want from *me*?"

"Honesty, common purpose, comfort, love. Nothing more.

Nothing less," I add meaningfully.

"Are you sure you're ready to give me that? Are you going to turn the job down?"

His question, the flippancy of it, takes me aback. "Is that a condition for you to give me those things?"

"No. But I don't see how you can expect me to be your man if you work for me."

"Well, clearly you can't be if I do."

"Then don't take the job."

His words are a slap in the face. "What?"

"I'm just saying, there are other jobs like that, right?"

"No there aren't. In fact, it's such a rare thing, only companies Wilde's size can support such a specific role. This is what I've been working for my whole life."

He looks at me like I sprouted a tail. "Are you saying *I* should turn the job down? You can't possibly expect me to do that. I've been working toward this *my* whole life."

"So have I," I retort.

"It's my family's company. I'm going to run it one day."

"That doesn't make it any less important to me, Tyson. And if I can't expect you to turn it down how can you expect me to?"

He gives a sharp sigh of frustration and starts to pace. "Okay, then…we'll just have to be discreet. But Dina, we can't stop what we just started."

"We didn't *just* start. We've been doing this thing for more than two years, Tyson. This weekend was a reset, with an escape hatch."

"And what? You want to use it?"

I certainly don't want to. But…I want to take him home to meet my dad. I want his family to know we're together. And that he asked me to do what he isn't willing to feels too familiar and terrible.

"Tyson, I have to go." I walk back into the bedroom and start rifling around for my underwear.

"Wait, what? When is your train?"

I tug on my bra and panties and slip on my shoes. "I don't know. I need to book it. All my stuff is still back at Le Meurice. I hope it's okay. I was supposed to check out yesterday and be back in London today. And you've got to get to work too. They probably think you're dead."

He pulls on a T-shirt and a pair of jeans. "Dina, we were talking."

"I know. But I've seen this movie before, I know what happens next, so I just want to skip to the credits."

"What movie? What are you talking about?"

"I put my career on hold to follow him all over the world while he pursued opportunities that he said were once in a lifetime. I didn't want to move every year, but we were married, and I wanted him to have that. But as soon as I asked for the same consideration, he refused."

"Ah, and there's your first mistake, grasshopper. You shouldn't give with the expectation of getting something back."

I grind my teeth together, frustrated at his making light of what feels like an existential crisis

"*That* is utter bullshit. Yesterday, you said you loved those mushrooms. But in truth, you just enjoy them. 'Cause if you had to grow them to keep eating them, I doubt you would. Which is fine. It just means it's not your passion."

"I'm missing something, Dina. Why the hell are we talking about mushrooms?"

I groan, frustrated that I have to spell it out. "I want someone who will do the work and not just enjoy the harvest. And I want to be with someone who's worth the work I put in, too."

"How, when you won't give anyone a chance?"

"I've given you so many chances. You had one just now."

"That's not what a chance looks like. You can't possibly expect me to consider it."

I glower at him. "Yes, how *silly* of me to expect Tyson Wilde to give as good as he expects to get." I half laugh, half sob and brush the tears off my cheek.

"Dina. Come on."

"No. It's for the best. And at least neither of us have to worry about losing our dream jobs."

He sits back down on the bed and stares at the floor but doesn't say a word.

"I'm gonna go," I mutter.

"Let me call you a car," he offers. But his voice is listless, and I can tell he doesn't want to.

"I'm going to walk. I'll be fine, and you need to get ready for work."

He stands and grabs my shoulders, shaking me slightly with the force of the movement. "So that's it? You're just going to leave? After you set a damn fire in my heart and let me think I'd finally started to warm yours up?"

"I set a fire in your heart?"

He presses a kiss to my mouth and pulls me into a hug. And I swear, the ground beneath my feet quakes when he whispers, "It's an inferno, and it's hot enough to keep us both warm. Trust me."

20

The Legend
Tyson

"How was your weekend?" Remi asks when I answer his call. I decided to work from home today. But all I've done is sit at my desk and replay my conversation with Dina. She's been gone for six hours, and it feels like a week. "She's gone, Remi. I fucked up."

He chuckles. "I thought Dupont signed the deal, and who's gone?"

"Never mind." I forgot how clueless Remi is when it comes to the rest of our personal lives.

"No, not never mind. Tell me. Wait, is this about Dina?"

"I don't want to talk about it. And why can't any of you just mind your own business?"

"Are you looking in the mirror right now? You could have written a sibling's manual on snooping and interfering."

"Why are you calling me? Shouldn't you be in court or something?"

"It's six a.m. here, and I was calling you to find out how your weekend was and to congratulate you on the job. Mom said it's yours for the taking."

"Only because she's desperate." I flop onto my bed.

"Tyson, you know she values you. Hell, she credits your strategy for singlehandedly growing Wilde's retail distribution last year. You're her rainmaker."

"And yet I wasn't the best candidate for the job until suddenly I was the only choice."

"Woah. Ty, that's not true."

"It is, and when I step into that role and crush it, she'll be forced to admit she was wrong."

"Let me give you some advice, you can take it as you will."

"Go ahead." I normally chafe against his efforts to "school me," a reflex from a childhood spent living in his shadow. But right now, I'm hungry for his help.

He's silent for a few seconds, and I know he's thinking, choosing his words. So I wait patiently, because I know he's about to lay some wisdom on me. "Instead of beating your head against the brick wall of our mother's unknowable motivations and unshakeable fidelity to Wilde World, you're missing out on the things that are actually meant for you."

"What if you'd had to choose between your firm and Kal?"

"I'd set the place on fire myself." He says it with no hint of humor or levity in his voice.

"Really?"

"Oh, trust me. I can build another company in what's left of my lifetime. Maybe not back to what Wilde Law is now, but I could do it. But I could never find another woman made so perfectly for me than my wife."

"And you know she loves you. I don't know how Dina feels. And I'm crazy about her, but what if she's not the one?"

"There's no magical *the one*. There's two people deciding they love each other enough to do hard things with, to make sacrifices for, to forgive. And then there's everyone else. And if you're so sure you're meant to run Wilde, then you shouldn't be afraid to let it go until the time is right."

His words wash over me and sink in, but it's not my job or my mother or even my damn pride they make me think of.

It's Dina, and how today, when I let her leave, as much as I hated to let her go, I wasn't afraid to. Because through word and deed, she's shown that I don't need to be. I know my heart is safe with her. I know we'll find a way. Now I just need her to know it, too.

* * * *

"No. Absolutely not. It's a liability, Ty, not happening." My mother's gaze is unwavering through the screen of my phone.

I knew she'd say no, but I had to try because this isn't going to be easy. But it'll be worth it.

"So there's no wiggle room. Either she goes, or I do?"

"Unfortunately."

"Could you at least pretend you care?"

"Tyson, do I look like a bag of salt? Of course, I care. And I'm not telling you that you can't be with Dina if you want to. But one of you must leave your role. And I want you to think about this honestly, are you sure you're ready for a relationship? You were a sworn bachelor a week ago."

My blood boils.

"You don't get to code switch from mother to boss like that. My personal life isn't Tina Wilde CEO's business. I don't want to talk to her about it. I just told you I want to be in a relationship with Dina. And you know what? I want that more than I want to keep toiling for your respect."

Her eyes darken like thunderclouds. "Tyson Wilde." My name cracks like lightning from her lips. "I don't care what you call me, I am always your mother, and you need to watch how you talk to me. I may have not been a perfect parent, but I've certainly earned that."

"I'm sorry."

"And as for toiling for my respect, you've had that since the day you drew breath. Do you know what a miracle you are? I would have died if I hadn't needed to stay alive for you. You saved me. And you are the very last good thing your father ever gave me."

"Really?"

"Oh, Tyson. Come on. Give me some credit. I'm hard on you because I need to be."

"I feel like you've never forgiven me for what happened with Kayleigh." I hate to even say the name of the woman that led me to the wilderness of self-doubt and tunnel vision.

"What? That was so long ago."

"Well, I remember it like it was yesterday. You said I was, and I quote, 'as weak-willed as my father.'"

Her mouth falls open. "No. I didn't."

"Oh, trust me, you did."

She blows out a harsh breath. "Tyson, I'm so sorry. I was angry and said things I didn't mean. That was one of those times, because I know you'd never do what he did. You're a good man who is loyal and constant to the people you love. I was hard on you, but only because I knew you could do it. And you've more than proven yourself."

"So why did you hire Erin instead of me?"

"Oh, for God's sake. It's been more than a year." She sits back in her chair as if she's exhausted.

"It feels like yesterday. Maybe it's because that's when you made me feel like the kid who only gets picked for the team 'cause there's no one else."

She gasps and reaches for her chest. "That is not true. I've told you a thousand times, Erin was a better fit at the time."

"And why now?"

"We'd be lucky to have you and… I thought it would make you happy."

"That is a terrible reason," I snap.

She purses her lips. "Of course, you focus on the last part and ignore how I started with we'd be lucky to have you. You'd be great at it, but Tyson, you'd be bored. But if it's what you want, I don't want to stand in your way. Even though I'm afraid you'll be bored and ready to leave in a few months. And I really don't want to have to fill this role twice in two years."

"Why do you think I'll be bored?"

"Because I know you better than you know yourself."

"Right. I don't think so."

"Have *you* ever seen your own asshole?"

"No."

"Exactly. I'm your mother, and I know. I also think you're ready to leave the nest. So much so I'm tempted to give you a shove."

I look at her, astonished by the smile on her face as she says it. "Are you…firing me?"

She folds her hands in front of her. "I'm not firing you, Tyson. I'm just saying that if you want to date Dina, one of you will have to go. And I think it should be you."

"Wow, that's nice."

She gives a short lift of her eyebrows, unapologetic and unmoved. "She was made for this work. And she's really earned it."

"So have I."

"You can do better. And that name is yours whether you work here or not. You don't have to prove you're one of us."

I think about what she's saying. But I need to sleep on it.

"What time is Dina coming in?"

"Nine."

"I'll be there at eight. And I'll have an answer for you then."

I hang up, and the answer is so clear, I can't believe I didn't see it all along.

I hope I'm not too late.

21

Back Where It Started
Dina

When I step off the elevator onto Tina Wilde's floor, I'm moving by the sheer force of my will. Halfway back to London, I started to panic. I was so triggered by Tyson's suggestion that I not take the job that I didn't stop to listen when he asked me to.

I'm so used to wishing for things I can't have that I've forgotten what it feels like to be satisfied. And as much as I've asked him to show me, I've never really told him how much he means to me.

But I'm going to today. As soon as I meet Mrs. Wilde and figure out whether the job is still mine for the taking.

I knock lightly on the door.

"Come in, Dina."

I take a deep breath and push the doors open and stop short when I see Tyson getting up from one of the teal blue chairs on the other side of his mother's desk. The smile on his face when he sees me makes me want to run and throw my arms around his neck and tell him I'm sorry I left him.

"Hi. What are you doing here?"

"We just finished our meeting. I'll leave so you can have yours." He heads toward the door.

"No." I rush to stand in front of him. "Please, if it's okay, I'd like you to stay. If that's okay?" I glance at Mrs. Wilde.

"I don't have an issue. Tyson?"

"If you want me to stay, sure." His expression is unreadable as he takes his seat again.

I sit and address Mrs. Wilde. "I know you called me here to talk about the Dupont deal and the job offer you made. But first I have to confess that I lied to you when we talked."

"I know," she says flatly.

I frown dubiously. "You know *what?*"

"That you were with Tyson. That you had been all weekend."

"I told her," Tyson says.

I keep my eyes on Mrs. Wilde. "I'm sorry I didn't tell you the truth about that, but I wasn't thinking clearly, and I was exhausted. I used poor judgment. We both did."

I glance at Tyson, hoping he's not glaring at me. Instead, he's watching me with an expression I've never seen before in his eyes. Like he wants to run into my arms, too.

"Can you stare at each other when the meeting is over?"

Heat blooms from the back of my neck to the tips of my ears, but I keep my game face on and nod. "I let you believe before I left for Paris that I was indifferent to him."

"Well, I knew you weren't indifferent. I thought you just didn't like him."

I laugh at her blunt words. "Oh, I liked him plenty—too much, in fact. And I should have told you that there were some unresolved feelings between us. But I thought he would be indifferent to *me.*"

I can feel Tyson's eyes on me, but I don't dare look at him before I'm done saying what I came to. "And yesterday I agreed to complete a task that I knew I wouldn't be able to. In order to avoid telling you that I was with him. I admire and respect you tremendously, and I'm sorry I let my personal feelings get ahead of my professional responsibilities. But I also can't promise it won't happen again. Because I'm falling in love with him, and I'll want to protect him. So that means whether Tyson is in my reporting hierarchy or not, I'm not sure I can be objective when it comes to him." Saying it aloud for the first time is like taking a deep breath after choking on smoke.

"Dina—"

"No don't say anything yet, Tyson, I wa—"

"Dammit, Dina." He raises his voice, and I realize with a start that he's never done so before. Not even when he got in Ron's face at dinner. Mrs. Wilde looks surprised, too.

He clears his throat and adjusts the cuff of his shirt. "I know I shouldn't expect you to trust me overnight. And yes, I *am* afraid of messing up, not being good at being your man. But you're so afraid of being let down that you don't give people the chance to even try."

I nod, my throat clogged by tears. He's paid such close to attention to me, and I feel so seen, so understood. "Yes, I know. It's easier that way."

"No, Dina. It's not." Mrs. Wilde's words are a sharp admonishment, and she's watching me with a thoughtful expression in her dark eyes as she steeples her fingers beneath her chin. "It's just a different kind of hard. And dare I say, a much less rewarding one. Yes, some people are going to let you down. Because…"

"They're people," Tyson finishes the sentence for her, and they share a smile that tells me it's a private joke.

"And yes, it will mean hurt, disruption, but you'll survive. And you'll get better at knowing who and what to put your faith in. And there's no better feeling than having your faith rewarded. But it'll never happen if you don't give it a chance to," Mrs. Wilde says.

"I know I messed up. But baby, I'm right here with you in this," Tyson calling me baby is enough to make me melt and forget where I am.

I reach for his hand and search his face. "You are?"

He smiles and grasps my hand. "Yes, Dina. I am."

Oh God, is this for real? Am I about to have what I want and what I need all at once?

Mrs. Wilde clears her throat. "Well, that's very, very good news. And I'm so glad that at least one of my sons has good taste in women."

"Mom," Tyson scolds. She and Kal had a rocky start to their relationship that never quite smoothed out, but I suspect she says things like that to be provoking more than anything.

"Have you come to resign?" The tight clip in her voice and the direct nature of her words bring me crashing back down to earth.

My eyes widen. "No, I haven't." I turn to Tyson, who is staring at me incredulously. "I'm sorry, Ty, but I'm not going to resign. I don't expect you will either."

I look back at Mrs. Wilde. "I was going to propose that we present a cost benefit analysis of our roles. May the best person win. If that's not me, I'll be the first one to toast Tyson. Because I know if I gave him the chance, he'd do the same for me."

She smiles and glances up at the ceiling. "I'll leave you two alone now. Dina, I'll see you in Houston in a few months. Tyson, plan to spend the next few days here."

She pats me on the shoulder and mutters, "Thank the Lord" before she strides out and leaves us alone.

"Why is she saying thank the lord?" I jump out of my seat and stand in front of him.

He cups me around the waist. "Because, you sweet thing, I turned the job down this morning."

"You did?" I stare down at him, dazed.

"And gave my three-month notice for my position in France."

"You did what? Why?" I lean away from him, trying to make sense of the words he's saying and the thousand-watt smile on his face.

He tugs me into his lap. "How can I woo you and convince you to be mine if I'm in France and you're in Houston?"

He leans down to kiss me. I put my hand on his chest to stop him. "I thought you wanted that job more than anything."

"Turns out we were both wrong."

He leans down to kiss me again, and this time I let him. I've missed him so much. How did I live months without this? "Oh, Tyson, are you sure?"

"I've been ready to leave France since a month after I got there. If I wanted the COO job enough to duke it out with you, I would. And if you came out the victor, I'd be the first one to buy you champagne, too."

"I don't want you to give it up for me."

"I want there to be an us. I'm not giving up anything I can't find somewhere else. And you, my beautiful Huntress, broke the mold. You're irreplaceable."

I blink rapidly to clear the tears that pool without warning. "Are you ready? Really?"

"This weekend, when we were working together, I felt unstoppable. I want that feeling all the time. And when I feel lost, I know you'll leave the light on so I can find my way home. I want to try. If *you're* ready to let me. *Please,* let me."

My heart feels so full, I'm afraid it will burst. "Yes, I am. So ready."

"Listen, you know if you give me half a chance, I'll catch you and I'm never going to let you go. I mean that."

"How about we just start with dinner?" I ask with a giddy giggle.

"How about you let me kiss you like I've been dying to?"

"Not in my office." Mrs. Wilde's disembodied voice fills the room.

"What the hell?" Tyson sits up and glances around the room.

"She has cameras, and microphones." I speak in a hushed voice.

"It would serve her right if we had sex right here," he whispers in my ear.

"But it serves us *better* to wait until we're back at my hotel."

He grins at me. "Us. I like the sound of that. I don't know why I was worried about this relationship stuff. We're going to crush it."

We so are. Because that's what we do. And cameras be damned, I wrap my arm around his neck and pull his lips to mine. "But first, kiss me like you've been dying to."

Epilogue

The Perfect Ending
Dina
Two Years Later

Mrs. Wilde's wedding was supposed to be the event of the season when her engagement was announced. But the world had other ideas. Two natural disasters and a worldwide pandemic later, the bride and groom were married in a small outdoor ceremony that was the definition of a family affair.

She was escorted down a grassy aisle by her youngest son, and the ceremony was officiated by her oldest one. Her daughter was her matron of honor. Her two granddaughters, her flower girls. She wore a custom Eki Orleans gown and a coronet of white roses in her hair.

She and Max exchanged their vows under the huge magnolia tree in the center of the green courtyard of Rivers Wilde. Tyson sat next to me, holding my hand so tightly it hurt as he watched his mother pledge her heart and soul to the love of her life. And there wasn't a dry eye in the crowd as they walked down the aisle again, holding hands and bound forever.

I watched it all with a sense of hope. If after everything she's been through, she can find her fairytale ending, then I know that Tyson and I will be just fine.

"You want anything else to eat?"

"Speak of the devil and he will appear," I quip and move to make room for Tyson on the small love seat I curled up on an hour ago.

"You okay? Tired?" He lifts my feet onto his lap and runs his knuckle down my arch. I moan and smile.

"That feels so good. Yes, I'm tired. How are you not?"

"Oh, I am, but those kids don't give a damn. The only reason I'm not still running after them is 'cause they started bringing out slices of cake."

I sit up. "No way. And you walked over here to see me with no cake in hand? Sometimes I think you don't know me at all."

"It has gluten, babe."

I stop midrise and pout. "Well, damn," I grumble and sit back down.

"Oh, don't you worry, I've got some back at the house. Sweet made it just for you. Same flavors and everything."

"She did? I don't think she likes me," I say of the woman who owns the coffee shop and bakery in the enclave.

Tyson grimaces. "I mean…you didn't exactly ingratiate yourself with her when you made that crack about Ghana jollof being better than Nigerian jollof."

I hang my head and groan at the memory. "It is. And if I'd known she was from Nigeria, I wouldn't have said it."

"She said it was fine, D, it's okay."

"No, what she said is, 'You're ignorant, so I forgive you.'"

He chuckles. "Yeah, she sure did. But it doesn't matter. She *loves* me, and we're a package deal." He links our fingers and tugs me to my feet. "Come on, let's go say our goodbyes and go home."

Tyson was right, we crushed this relationship thing. He stepped down from his role in Paris exactly three months after he gave his notice. Leaving Wilde World was like a dam bursting. He set up his marketing consulting business and hit the ground running. Wilde World is one of his clients, and I do a little work for him, too.

Tyson told me he loved me three weeks after that meeting in his mother's office..

He looked as surprised by it as I was to hear it, but then, he couldn't stop saying it.

It was like he was making up for lost time.

I'm not complaining, I'd like it if he said it at the end of every sentence. Because that's how often I think it.

But we took everything else slowly. Until we were facing separation when the whole world went into quarantine and we decided to move in together instead. We bought a town house in the Ivy, and I was so nervous that it would be too much commitment too soon.

But like everything else he puts his mind to, he's thriving in his role as partner. There haven't been any more grand gestures like quitting his job, but there are fresh flowers every morning and Bissap every weekend. He learned enough Vietnamese to greet my father properly the first time they met. Not that my dad would have held it against him, but that he made the effort made him an instant Tyson fan.

But no one is a bigger fan of him than me. All of him. He's a hard nut to crack, and I've got to be on my game when we go toe-to-toe about anything. We pick our battles—and sometimes die on separate hills.

But we haven't spent a night apart since he moved to Houston because the one thing we never disagree on is that we're much happier together than apart.

As settled as we feel, this is just the beginning of our journey. I know my daredevil will still take risks and do reckless things, but he can also take care of my heart. And I'm finally ready to let him.

* * * *

Want to read an extended epilogue? Well, you're in luck. You can find it here: http://bit.ly/DareDevil_Extra

Author's Note

Dear reader,

I hope you loved this visit to Rivers Wilde. I created this series after watching an episode of Anthony Bourdain's show, Parts Unknown, that was set here.

I grew up in Houston, but I've lived away for almost 20 years when I moved back to be closer to my parents again. I watched that show and realized that I'd forgotten what brought, and kept, my parents to this city 37 years ago when they left their home in Ghana in pursuit of better opportunities for their three young daughters.

They chose Houston because it is brimming with opportunity and is truly America's melting pot. I wanted to create a world that reflected that. Houston is a sprawling urban landscape that more than two million people call home, and so I created a "small town" like enclave that I named Rivers Wilde.

And in it, I placed people from all over the world, of all walks of life and made a utopia where they all work toward the common purpose of building a community.

The Daredevil is the 5th book in the series. But there's a whole world to explore, and I'm just getting started.

You can learn more about the series and the characters in it by visiting riverswilde.com.

I hope you love it here and thank you so much for reading.

PS - The joke at the end about Ghana Jollof and Nigerian Jollof is an inside joke between two rival (friendly) West African countries that is always a heated debate at parties. This article will tell you more about it if you're interested: http://bit.ly/DD_JollofWars

Wishing your wildest dreams come true,

Dylan

Sign up for the 1001 Dark Nights Newsletter and be entered to win a Tiffany Key necklace.

There's a contest every month!

Go to www.1001DarkNights.com to subscribe.

As a bonus, all subscribers can download FIVE FREE exclusive books!

Discover 1001 Dark Nights Collection Eight

DRAGON REVEALED by Donna Grant
A Dragon Kings Novella

CAPTURED IN INK by Carrie Ann Ryan
A Montgomery Ink: Boulder Novella

SECURING JANE by Susan Stoker
A SEAL of Protection: Legacy Series Novella

WILD WIND by Kristen Ashley
A Chaos Novella

DARE TO TEASE by Carly Phillips
A Dare Nation Novella

VAMPIRE by Rebecca Zanetti
A Dark Protectors/Rebels Novella

MAFIA KING by Rachel Van Dyken
A Mafia Royals Novella

THE GRAVEDIGGER'S SON by Darynda Jones
A Charley Davidson Novella

FINALE by Skye Warren
A North Security Novella

MEMORIES OF YOU by J. Kenner
A Stark Securities Novella

SLAYED BY DARKNESS by Alexandra Ivy
A Guardians of Eternity Novella

TREASURED by Lexi Blake
A Masters and Mercenaries Novella

THE DAREDEVIL by Dylan Allen
A Rivers Wilde Novella

BOND OF DESTINY by Larissa Ione
A Demonica Novella

THE CLOSE-UP by Kennedy Ryan
A Hollywood Renaissance Novella

MORE THAN POSSESS YOU by Shayla Black
A More Than Words Novella

HAUNTED HOUSE by Heather Graham
A Krewe of Hunters Novella

MAN FOR ME by Laurelin Paige
A Man In Charge Novella

THE RHYTHM METHOD by Kylie Scott
A Stage Dive Novella

JONAH BENNETT by Tijan
A Bennett Mafia Novella

CHANGE WITH ME by Kristen Proby
A With Me In Seattle Novella

THE DARKEST DESTINY by Gena Showalter
A Lords of the Underworld Novella

Also from Blue Box Press

THE LAST TIARA by M.J. Rose

THE CROWN OF GILDED BONES by Jennifer L. Armentrout
A Blood and Ash Novel

THE MISSING SISTER by Lucinda Riley

THE END OF FOREVER by Steve Berry and M.J. Rose
A Cassiopeia Vitt Adventure

THE STEAL by C. W. Gortner and M.J. Rose

CHASING SERENITY by Kristen Ashley
A River Rain Novel

A SHADOW IN THE EMBER by Jennifer L. Armentrout
A Flesh and Fire Novel

The Legacy
Rivers Wilde Book 1
By Dylan Allen
Now available!

"Toe curling chemistry, a sexy alpha male, and a smart heroine! The Legacy is **EPIC! Hands down, one of my fav reads this year!**"-- Ilsa Madden Mills, *Wall Street Journal* Bestselling Author.

He just won control of his legacy. Loving her could cost him everything.

Billionaire Hayes Rivers came into my life like a hurricane...

Heir to an oil empire, he was sexy and seductive, controlling and scorching hot. I craved every touch, every filthy promise that fell from his beautiful mouth, knowing he could break me. My past had left me battered and bruised, with scars he was determined to heal.

Loving him was like drowning—he consumed me, body and soul.

But Hayes has secrets of his own. And nothing could prepare me for the shocking pieces of our pasts that threaten to rip us apart.

When the truth is revealed will our love be enough to shelter the storm?

* * * *

"*Who* is *that?*" I lean over to Cass and whisper without taking my eyes off the tall, well-built, beautiful man who just strode into the tent like he's about to tell us all he's our new ruler and ask us to pledge our loyalty or die. He's even more beautiful in that suit than he was in that hallway this afternoon. I can still feel the soft brush of his fingers on my neck. The way my breath caught in my throat when he'd dragged the pendant up my chest until it nestled into the small hollow at the base of my throat.

His dark, wavy hair is just long enough to curl right at the edge of his crisp white tuxedo shirt. It's unruly and perfectly artless in a way that no human hand, and no amount of pomade, could create. Those silky dark-chocolate waves are the work of God himself. His profile is strong and bold; his nose prominent and straight. His lips are set in a straight line but I can see their fullness even in his profile. And God, his jaw. It's chiseled and wide and covered in a beard low enough to be a five o'clock shadow, meticulously groomed so you can tell it's not. His broad, tall frame is poured into a black tuxedo that fits him perfectly. He looks like he's the sovereign of something—a country, a business, a thousand women in a harem somewhere…

Heads turn as he crosses the room. And I can't blame them—not even a little bit. He oozes sex and power. His long strides eat up the floor, and he reaches the lone empty table at the back of the tent quickly. When he's adorned the chair with his glorious body, he turns to face the front of the room where the bridal party is sitting and giving their speeches.

"Who's who?" she asks and pokes her head around the room. I tug her arm and nod at him.

"Him. Also known as the man of all of my dirty dreams," I purr excitedly, my eyes trained on the finest specimen of man I've ever seen this close up.

"Ohhh," she drawls, eyes widening with interest and props her chin on her hand and ogles him.

"That's Hayes Rivers," the woman on my right says. Cass and I both turn to face her, surprised by her interjection.

"Heir to Kingdom," she says when neither of us respond.

"I knew it. He looks like a king. Which kingdom?" I ask. I'm already imagining myself in a ball gown, crown on my head walking down some long, red-carpeted aisle where he's waiting at the end.

"No, not *a kingdom*." And just like that, she kills my dream. "*Kingdom* is the name of his family's business. He inherited all the money when he turned twenty-five. And now he's the new Rivers king," she says.

"How old is he now?" I ask, my curiosity overtaking my normal abhorrence for gossip.

"He must be thirty…he's one of the richest men in the freaking world," she exclaims.

"Really? Why's he here?"

"His grandmother is friends with the groom," our little canary says. "I can't believe you've never heard of him. His return to Houston is all anyone's talking about," she says and looks at both of us like we're crazy.

"I don't live in Houston," I say.

"Well, *I* heard…" Her eyes dart around as if checking for spies and then she leans into us. "Apparently, he had a fight with his ex. And it got *physical*," she grimaces. But her eyes are twinkling. "I'm not one to gossip…" she says, and Cass and I exchange a *yeah, right* look.

"She was all over the place, and always wearing sunglasses. No one saw her eyes, mind you, and she never said so but it was *obvious* what she was hiding. He roughed her up," she says.

My brain, offended by the lack of logic in her words forces my gaze away from the delicious man and onto the source of its ire. There's no warmth in them when they land on her and her silly, careless smile falters.

"That's actually the exact opposite of obvious," I say dismissively.

"Only if you're blind. I mean, yeah, he's nice to look at, but he seems so…*angry*, don't you think?"

I glance at him, and just then, like he knows what she said, his jaw clenches.

"Well, if people were talking about me like this, I might be angry, too."

The woman snorts a derisive laugh. "You think you know better, go ahead and ignore me. But don't say you weren't warned," she says and turns back to the victim on her other side.

As if I need any warning. I can smell a violent man the minute he enters the room. I grew up with them under the same roof. I watched them do more damage than any of the natural disasters that were a way of life for us in the Mississippi Delta.

I lean toward Cass. "He's staying on our floor," I whisper. I can't take my eyes off him and just the sight of him makes my whole body tingle.

"Thank you, God," I say, pressing my hands together in gratitude.

Cass laughs. "I mean, he does clean up nicely, but he looks like he'd be more comfortable in a boxing ring than on a dance floor," she says.

"Yes, exactly," I practically purr before I take another sip of my gin and tonic. My thighs clench when I think about how rough things could get.

"His nose doesn't look like it's been broken, though," she muses.

"No one's perfect," I joke and take a final swig of my drink.

"Enjoy. My fantasy Italian fling is more in the style of Jude Law in the *Talented Mr. Ripley*. He looks like he could eat Jude Law in a single bite."

"Or me," I drawl with a wink and stand. Cass grabs my arm and yanks me back down in my seat. "Where in the world are you going? You are *not* going to approach him," she says as if scandalized.

"I am *so* going to approach him. I stand again.

She gasps, "Who *are* you?"

I glance over at her and grin at her wide-eyed expression. "I'm Confidence Ryan, and I'm about to climb my very own Mt. Olympus."

About Dylan Allen

Wall Street Journal and USA Today Bestselling Author, Dylan Allen writes compelling, dramatic, emotional romances with exceptional, diverse characters you'll root for and never forget

A self-proclaimed happily ever junkie, she loves creating stories where her characters find a love worth fighting for. When she isn't writing or reading, eating, or cooking, Dylan indulges her wanderlust by planning her next globe-trotting adventure.

Dylan was born in Accra, Ghana (West Africa) but was raised in Houston, Texas. Dylan is a proud graduate of Tufts University, Howard University School of Law and the London School of Economics and Political Science. After twenty years of adventure and wild oat sowing, Dylan, her amazing husband and two incredible children returned to Houston where they now make their home.

* * * *

I love to hear from readers! email me at Dylan@dylanallenbooks.com

Are you on Facebook? Join my private reader group, Dylan's Day Dreamers. It's where I spend most of my time online and it's a lot of fun!

Discover 1001 Dark Nights

THE ONLY ONE by Lauren Blakely ~ SWEET SURRENDER by
Liliana Hart

COLLECTION FOUR
ROCK CHICK REAWAKENING by Kristen Ashley ~ ADORING
INK by Carrie Ann Ryan ~ SWEET RIVALRY by K. Bromberg ~
SHADE'S LADY by Joanna Wylde ~ RAZR by Larissa Ione ~
ARRANGED by Lexi Blake ~ TANGLED by Rebecca Zanetti ~
HOLD ME by J. Kenner ~ SOMEHOW, SOME WAY by Jennifer
Probst ~ TOO CLOSE TO CALL by Tessa Bailey ~ HUNTED by
Elisabeth Naughton ~ EYES ON YOU by Laura Kaye ~ BLADE by
Alexandra Ivy/Laura Wright ~ DRAGON BURN by Donna Grant ~
TRIPPED OUT by Lorelei James ~ STUD FINDER by Lauren Blakely
~ MIDNIGHT UNLEASHED by Lara Adrian ~ HALLOW BE THE
HAUNT by Heather Graham ~ DIRTY FILTHY FIX by Laurelin
Paige ~ THE BED MATE by Kendall Ryan ~ NIGHT GAMES by CD
Reiss ~ NO RESERVATIONS by Kristen Proby ~ DAWN OF
SURRENDER by Liliana Hart

COLLECTION FIVE
BLAZE ERUPTING by Rebecca Zanetti ~ ROUGH RIDE by Kristen
Ashley ~ HAWKYN by Larissa Ione ~ RIDE DIRTY by Laura Kaye ~
ROME'S CHANCE by Joanna Wylde ~ THE MARRIAGE
ARRANGEMENT by Jennifer Probst ~ SURRENDER by Elisabeth
Naughton ~ INKED NIGHTS by Carrie Ann Ryan ~ ENVY by
Rachel Van Dyken ~ PROTECTED by Lexi Blake ~ THE PRINCE by
Jennifer L. Armentrout ~ PLEASE ME by J. Kenner ~ WOUND
TIGHT by Lorelei James ~ STRONG by Kylie Scott ~ DRAGON
NIGHT by Donna Grant ~ TEMPTING BROOKE by Kristen Proby
~ HAUNTED BE THE HOLIDAYS by Heather Graham ~
CONTROL by K. Bromberg ~ HUNKY HEARTBREAKER by
Kendall Ryan ~ THE DARKEST CAPTIVE by Gena Showalter

COLLECTION SIX
DRAGON CLAIMED by Donna Grant ~ ASHES TO INK by Carrie
Ann Ryan ~ ENSNARED by Elisabeth Naughton ~ EVERMORE by
Corinne Michaels ~ VENGEANCE by Rebecca Zanetti ~ ELI'S
TRIUMPH by Joanna Wylde ~ CIPHER by Larissa Ione ~
RESCUING MACIE by Susan Stoker ~ ENCHANTED by Lexi Blake

~ TAKE THE BRIDE by Carly Phillips ~ INDULGE ME by J. Kenner ~ THE KING by Jennifer L. Armentrout ~ QUIET MAN by Kristen Ashley ~ ABANDON by Rachel Van Dyken ~ THE OPEN DOOR by Laurelin Paige ~ CLOSER by Kylie Scott ~ SOMETHING JUST LIKE THIS by Jennifer Probst ~ BLOOD NIGHT by Heather Graham ~ TWIST OF FATE by Jill Shalvis ~ MORE THAN PLEASURE YOU by Shayla Black ~ WONDER WITH ME by Kristen Proby ~ THE DARKEST ASSASSIN by Gena Showalter

COLLECTION SEVEN
THE BISHOP by Skye Warren ~ TAKEN WITH YOU by Carrie Ann Ryan ~ DRAGON LOST by Donna Grant ~ SEXY LOVE by Carly Phillips ~ PROVOKE by Rachel Van Dyken ~ RAFE by Sawyer Bennett ~ THE NAUGHTY PRINCESS by Claire Contreras ~ THE GRAVEYARD SHIFT by Darynda Jones ~ CHARMED by Lexi Blake ~ SACRIFICE OF DARKNESS by Alexandra Ivy ~ THE QUEEN by Jen Armentrout ~ BEGIN AGAIN by Jennifer Probst ~ VIXEN by Rebecca Zanetti ~ SLASH by Laurelin Paige ~ THE DEAD HEAT OF SUMMER by Heather Graham ~ WILD FIRE by Kristen Ashley ~ MORE THAN PROTECT YOU by Shayla Black ~ LOVE SONG by Kylie Scott ~ CHERISH ME by J. Kenner ~ SHINE WITH ME by Kristen Proby

Discover Blue Box Press
TAME ME by J. Kenner ~ TEMPT ME by J. Kenner ~ DAMIEN by J. Kenner ~ TEASE ME by J. Kenner ~ REAPER by Larissa Ione ~ THE SURRENDER GATE by Christopher Rice ~ SERVICING THE TARGET by Cherise Sinclair ~ THE LAKE OF LEARNING by Steve Berry and MJ Rose ~ THE MUSEUM OF MYSTERIES by Steve Berry and MJ Rose ~ TEASE ME by J. Kenner ~ FROM BLOOD AND ASH by Jennifer L. Armentrout ~ QUEEN MOVE by Kennedy Ryan ~ THE HOUSE OF LONG AGO by Steve Berry and MJ Rose ~ THE BUTTERFLY ROOM by Lucinda Riley ~ A KINGDOM OF FLESH AND FIRE by Jennifer L. Armentrout

On Behalf of 1001 Dark Nights,

Liz Berry, M.J. Rose, and Jillian Stein would like to thank ~

Steve Berry
Doug Scofield
Benjamin Stein
Kim Guidroz
Social Butterfly PR
Ashley Wells
Asha Hossain
Chris Graham
Chelle Olson
Kasi Alexander
Jessica Johns
Dylan Stockton
Richard Blake
and Simon Lipskar

Made in the USA
Columbia, SC
28 July 2021